JATAKA TALES

Collection of stories related to the previous births of Lord Buddha

Compiled by
'KUNWAR' ANIL KUMAR

Edited by
ANURADHA SRIVASTAVA

MANOJ PUBLICATIONS

Publishers:

Manoj Publications
761, Main Road, Burari, Delhi-110084
Ph: 27611349, 27611116, Fax : 27611546
Mobile : 9868 112194
E-mail : info@manojpublications.com
Website : www.manojpublications.com

Showroom:
Manoj Publications
1583-84, Dariba Kalan, Chandni Chowk, Delhi-110006
Phone : 23262174, 23268216, Mobile : 9818753569

ISBN : 978-81-8133-469-5

₹ 80

Ninth Edition : 2012

Printers :
Jai Maya Offset
Jhilmil Industrial Area, Delhi-110095

Jataka Tales : *'Kunwar' Anil Kumar*

JATAKA TALES

'Jataka Tales' or 'Buddhistic Tales' relate to stories of the previous births of Lord Buddha. Lord Buddha having attained 'Wisdom' or 'All Knowingness' or after having had 'Self-Realisation' became capable of seeing through his previous births. He narrated these stories to his disciples, which became a source of learning social and moral values of life.

These are tales which had been told some more than two thousand years ago, aimed at uplifting people socially and morally. And one can expect to learn only good things from the lives of saints. For this simple reason we have made a judicious selection of such stories which may inculcate sublime virtues in the lives of our young readers.

A few other stories, not necessarily told by Lord Buddha, not necessarily related to his previous births, have also been included in this book for an added reading, designed to teach, and intended to convey instructions and information as well as pleasure and entertainment.

We, the publishers group, think, it is necessary for such books—meant for our young readers—to be didactic.

Now the responsibility lies with our young readers to tell us how successful we have been in our attempt.

— **Publishers**

CONTENTS

WISDOME AND ITS MIRACLE

A very-very long time ago, a farmer whose name was Ramsingh, lived in a village with his wife and child. Ramsingh himself was illiterate and poor, but he wanted to impart good education to his son, Sundar, so that his son did not have to work like a labourer like him throughout his life. He wanted his son to have good education and ultimately become a great support for their old age.

His son, Sundar was very intelligent and was being given education by Pandit Kastoorilal who lived in the same village. Sundar too, as his father had expected, wanted to become a big man after completing his education and bring every happiness in the lives of his parents.

As he was a boy of firm determination, he studied hard throughout the year and secured first position in his class. The whole village was full of praise for him. Ramsingh, his father, too was elated to know about the grand success of his son and was greatly overjoyed.

One night Ramsingh said to his wife, "You know, it's for a long time that I have been thinking of something for Sundar."

"Tell me!" said Ramsingh's wife. "What is it? Are you planning to get him married?"

"No, no, it's not that," said Ramsingh. "Of course, I shall get him married when the time comes; but for that he has to start earning independently. Anyway...right now I am thinking of sending him to town so that he learns some job-oriented skills and gets into some good trade. Because if I keep him with us in this village, he will remain a labourer only, like me. There is no scope in this village. Afterall his intelligence and education should be better utilized. As you already know, I don't even have a piece of land on which he could work and... bring prosperity to his life."

"I agree with you, but," said Ramsingh's wife, "Sundar has never been to a town. He doesn't know anyone there. Of course, he is intelligent and sensible; I am sure he can manage a good job also for himself in the town, but there should, at least, be some place where he can take shelter."

"Listen! I have a friend in the town. Though of course, we have not met each other during the last so many years, I am sure if Sundar goes and contacts him, he will not only give him shelter, he will manage to get him a good job also. He is a very good friend of mine," said Ramsingh with confidence.

"What you say is correct," Ramsingh's wife said, "but it's a tough decision. He has not been away from us even for a single day."

"It's your affection for Sundar that you are talking thus," said Ramsingh. "But in your heart of hearts, you too want your son to prosper. Come on! make yourself strong. Just imagine, if our Sundar goes to town and becomes a successful man, we shall have no problems. Our's will be a comfortable life when we become old."

And thus Ramsingh managed to make his wife agree on this point.

The same evening, when Sundar returned after playing with his friends, Ramsingh made him sit by his side with great affection and explained to him his plan.

Sundar became very happy to learn that his father wanted to send him to town.

In fact it was also Sunder's immense desire to go to town and earn so much that his parents got rid of poverty for ever.

Ramsingh's proposal had awakened his hopes. He said, "Father! I too was of the same view. I had a wish to go to town in search of some good job after completion of my studies, but thinking that you wouldn't allow me to leave this village, I had suppressed my wishes. But now since you yourself are willing to send me to town, there cannot be anything better for me. I am indeed very happy and shall definitely go to town to bring an end to our poverty."

Ramsingh explained to him the intricacies of the worldly affairs and bade him goodbye. But he didn't forget to give his friend's address to his son who lived in the town.

Sundar was a sensible boy. He was sensible enough to realise his parent's problems; he was also aware of the fact that if he remained in the village, he would have absolutely no future. It was his wish to become a successful man and bring every happines to his parents' life.

×   ×   ×

Sundar was dazzled to see the beauty of the town. He was amazed to see the shoulder-to-shoulder crowd of the town; something he had never seen before. The smallest shop in the town was bigger than the biggest shops in his village.

After having assuaged his curiosity with the beauty all around, Sundar set out in search of his father's friend's house.

But to his great disappointment, when he reached the destination, he was informed that his father's friend, Ramchandra had died a long time ago. The whereabouts of his family members could also not be found out. For a moment he became very nervous; but this was only momentary.

Hopes and despairs are two aspects of life; but Sundar was not one of those who would lose his nerve so easily. He was courageous and had a lot of confidence.

He consoled himself and mumbled, "Sundar, this is time when you must show courage and do something. Now since you have come to the town, you have to achieve your goal; no matter what it comes to; your father has great hopes of your doing well in the future. Don't you remember your teacher, Pandit Kastoorilal, Who used to say—'God helps those who help themselves'.

Consoling himself thus he began looking for an inn where he could settle down and plan for the future.

Fortunately, after a brief search, he found an inn, the owner of which, was an elderly person and a thorough gentleman. Sundar settled himself down, took bath and set out in search of job.

He contacted a number of shopkeepers in the town for a job. Every

shopkeeper was impressed by him; his appearance, his way of talking, everything made a mark. But, since he was an unknown figure in the town, none would offer him a job.

Thus, many days passed and Sundar was still jobless. The money he had brought from his village, too, was coming to an end. Sundar was desperately looking for some way to counter the situation.

He began thinking—'Alas! only if I knew someone in the town, I could have got a job.' One day, tired and desperate, he was sitting in the shade of a tree, contemplating his present circumstances. Not very far from there, were sitting two officials of the kingdom, having a chit-chat among themselves. One was saying to the other, "You may say anything, brother Ramvir! But you are very fortunate. We joined the service together, but you rose to the post of the king's treasurer and I started from the post of a constable and still am a constable only. This is called destiny."

"It's not destiny alone that matters; it's also one's wits and courage. I used my wits and remained honest in my dealing's with the king; and the king, seeing my honesty, made me his treasurer," said Ramvir.

"No, no, dear, I am sure you must have managed some amulet from some saint and, with the result, you have risen so high so soon. Brother! tell me the secret of your success," said the other one.

"That's the drawback," said Ramvir. "People like you, are always looking for some miracle to happen in their lives, so that they may get success without efforts. Look, if someone is courageous, honest and witty, he can do what is considered impossible. Do you see that dead mouse lying at the edge of the road.

"Yes, I can See."

"Do you see the passers-by seeing it, spitting at it with hatred and then going away?"

"Yes, I do see. But dear Ramvir! I am asking you the secret of your success and you are showing me a dead mouse. Isn't it funny?"

"Gangaram! Have patience. I am trying to tell you the secret of my success. Look, generally people would spit at that dead mouse and go away, but a person who is sensible and witty, would manage to earn some money out of the dead mouse also. Dear brother, it's the wit that brings you success; mantras and amulets have no role to play in one's life."

"Now, I understand, brother Ramvir," said a disappointed Gangaram. "In fact, you don't want to tell me the secret of your success. Never mind, a time will come when my days too will change. Let's leave now."

Both the officials got up and went away.

But Ramvir's words were still reverberating in the ears of Sundar.

He began thinking—'There is some meaning in what the treasurer has said. But who will by this dead mouse? How shall anyone earn money out of if?'

Sundar was staring at the dead mouse and contemplating this point, but he was not able to reach any conclusion.

Just then he saw a tonga coming on the road. A wealthy man was sitting in it with a cat in his lap. the cat was trying to escape from his clutches.

The tonga had just passed before the eyes of Sundar when the cat leapt from the lap of the wealthy man and entered the nearby bushes.

"Stop, stop! The cat has run away," shouted the wealthy man.

The Tonga stopped and the wealthy man rushed forth to catch the cat.

"O dear Tonga driver! My cat is hiding behind the bush. Please help me catch it." And then the wealthy man went and stood by the bushes and began calling, "Come, come, pussy come."

This was a funny scene for the passers-by. A big crowd had gathered around; the tonga driver and Sundar were also in the crowd.

"I was carrying this cat for a very special purpose. Someone please help me catch this cat." The wealthy man was pleading befor everyone.

The cat was in no mood to be caught again. She was baring her teeth in a furious snarl.

"Don't you see sir, how this cat is snarling? She is so furious that she will attack as soon as someone tries to catch her," said someone in the crowd.

Suddenly a bright idea flashed across the mind of Sundar. He said to the wealthy man, "Sir, I will do the job for you; but what will be my reward?"

"You mean to say that you will catch the cat? Oh dear boy! If you do it, I shall give you one silver coin in return," said th wealthy man joyfully.

"One silver coin!" Sundar was overjoyed. "All right! you please wait and see how I tame your cat.

Sundar ran to the other side of the road for the dead mouse. He said to himself, "Now I understand what the treasurer had meant when he said that a witty person could earn some money out of the dead mouse also.

He took a piece of string, formed a noose at one end of it and tied it round the neck of the dead mouse and came back.

"Move all of you please," he said to the crowd. "Please make a little space and the cat will come out.

"Oh, I had seen this dead mouse lying there," someone in the crowd said.

"This boy is very intelligent," said another one. "This is called— 'taking advantage of the situation'."

"I am sure this boy is destined to become a big man one day," said yet another one.

Sundar sat near the bushes and began dangling the dead mouse before the eyes of the cat.

The cat's mouth began watering to see the fat mouse dangling before her eyes. She looked at Sundar in a friendly way and began wagging her tail. Now she was purring and trying to come close to Sundar.

Everyone was watching with amazement. People in the crowd began laughing to see so drastic a change in the behaviour of the cat.

This allurement worked. The cat came out from behind the bushes; and as soon as she came out, Sundar began fondling her. He picked her up in his lap.

The cat began giving a low-pitched mew and looking at the dead mouse with an eagerness to devour it as soon as possible.

But Sundar did not allow the cat to get to the mouse; instead, he handed over both the cat and the mouse to the wealthy man and said, "Sir, so long as you have this mouse with you, this cat too will remain with you. She won't go anywhere. Now take care of her and give me my silver coin.

"Yes, yes! Why not." The wealthy man took out a silver coin from his pocket and gave it to Sundar. He said, "Young man, I have noticed that you have the capability of taking advantage of any situation, and I prophesy that you will rise to insurmountable heights one day, if you keep using your wits and wisdom thus.

"All I need is your blessings, sir," said an elated Sundar.

The crowd thinned out with words of praises for Sundar. Sundar was very happy that he had earned some money using his wit and wisdom for the first time in this town. He was looking at the silver coin again and again.

Sundar was thinking that it wouldn't be easy to get a job in that new town; so, why not do some business with the silver coin and multiply the amount.

Though of course, doing business with one silver coin—so meagre an amount—was not an easy job, still for a person like Sundar nothing was impossible.

First thing he did was to assuage his hunger. And then he began looking around with his sharp eyes, thinking what possible business could be done with the remaining amount. He was observing each and every thing very minutely.

It was summer season.

Wandering around he reached the royal garden; the garden was enormous in size, and hundreds of gardeners were working in it. Some labourers were busy in digging a foundation; perhaps the king had plans to build a new palace.

On the other side of the garden, there was a dense forest, where some woodcutters were felling trees. They were sweating like bullocks.

It was tremendously hot; even the water in the pond had become hot. The labourers, despite drinking water again and again, were not able to quench their thirst.

Seeing all this, an idea immediately flashed across Sundar's mind.

Sundar began thinking—'these poor labourers are getting restless due to excessive heat and, the hot water of the pond, can in no way quench their thirst. Their body is letting out the water, they are drinking, in the form of sweat, and the result is that they are as thirsty as they were. Under these circumstances, if they are given Sattu*, diluted in cold water, with jaggery, it will definitely make some difference and bring relief to them.

Thinking this, Sundar moved towards the market.

*ground flour of parched grains

13

He had enough money to buy a pitcher, Sattu and jaggery; and he did buy them all.

He diluted Sattu in cold water, came and sat outside the garden.

After some time the labourers, having finished their jobs, began coming out.

They were still terribly thirsty. They rushed forth as soon as they saw Sundar sitting with cold Sattu.

"Brother! Have you got something cold?" asked all of them in unison.

"Yes brothers! I have got cold Sattu and jaggery. Take as much as you want and quench your thirst," Sundar said with a sweet smile.

Sundar began giving diluted cold Sattu in tumblers and jaggery to everyone.

This indeed brought a great deal of relief to them.

After they were all fully satiated with cold Sattu, the chief of the gardeners said, "Brother! You have done us a great favour; we are indeed very greateful to you. Now it's our duty to give you something in return. How would you like to be repayed?"

"It's all up to you," said Sundar with all his simplicity. "It's not that I have done all this with any intentions of making profits; in fact, I was extremely pained to see all of you so restless with thirst. I wanted to bring relief to the labourers. Now I shall accept anything in return that you can give without taxing yourself.

"All right, my son! What we get as wages is only flowers. We sell them in the market and manage our bread and butter with the money we get. Since, we are poor people and have no money, each one of us will give you some flowers from his share, which you can sell in the market and earn some money," said the chief of the gardeners.

"As you wish," said Sundar.

The chief of the gardeners placed a basket before him and put in it a few flowers out of his share. Seeing the chief putting flowers in the basket, the gardeners also began giving parts of their shares.

And within no time the basket was full of flowers.

"Son! What's your good name?" asked the chief of the gardeners.

"I am Sundar."

"Sundar, you give us cold Sattu everyday and we shall give you flowers in returen. Thus, we shall have our thirst quenched and you will also earn some money everyday."

"All right, uncle!" said Sundar happily. "I take pleasure in serving others.

After, all the gardeners had gone, Sundar took the basketful of flowers on his head and the pitcher in his hand and left the place.

Earlier, while wandering around in search of job, he had seen a hillock also, on which there was a temple of Lord Shiva. The devotees of Lord Shiva used to collect there every evening for offering their worships.

Sharp as he was, Sundar decided to go and sell the flowers there.

He was extremely thankful to the dead mouse because of which he had succeeded in earning some money. The job may be big or small, but if someone is sincere, he is bound to get success.

Sundar went straight to the temple on the hillock and sat in a corner with his basket of flowers. There were others also selling

flowers, but their flowers were not as fresh as the flowers Sundar had brought. The result was that the devotees bought flowers from Sundar only, and within no time, Sundar had sold all his flowers and earned a lot of money.

Thus, Sundar earned one silver coin with the help of the dead mouse and then multiplied his earning to a great extent by using his wit and wisdom. And it was all because of the king's treasurer who had inadvertently brought the dead mouse to his notice. Neither would he have talked about the possibility of making some money out of the dead mouse, nor Sundar would have contemplated this point. And so, Sundar quietly accepted the treasurer as his mentor.

It was evening time. Sundar, who had lost his appetite due to failure in getting himself a job, suddenly began feeling very hungry. He came straight to the inn. The owner of the inn was seeing him so happy after a long time. He was an avuncular old man. Ever since Sundar had come to the town and stayed in his inn, the owner of the inn had started making enquiries about him, and having come to known that he had come to the town in search of some job and that he belonged to a poor family and was hardworking and industrious, he had developed a soft spot for him. He had begun treating Sundar as his own son. Whenever Sundar went out in search of job, the old man would pray for his success.

Today, when he saw Sundar happy and smiling, coming with a pitcher and a basket, he said, "What's the matter, Sundar? You look very happy today. I guess you have succeeded in getting a good job somewhere."

"I couldn't get any job, uncle," said Sundar putting his pitcher and the basket aside, "but I have definitely succeeded in starting a business with the help of a dead mouse."

"...business with the help of a dead mouse? I couldn't get it my son," said the old man.

Sundar sat by the side of the old man and gave a complete description of the whole day. The old man was extremely surprised to see his intelligence. "My son! this is miracle," said the old man. "You are sure to become a big man if you continue thus. All right! Go and get fresh and I shall get you something to eat. You must be hungry."

Sundar went in, took bath and ate to his fill. He was feeling very light and confident. Now he was sure that he won't have to starve in that town, and using his intelligence, he would be able to promote his business also.

Next day when Sundar woke up, he was in high spirits. Once again he diluted Sattu in cold water, filled his pitcher with it, and went and sat outside the garden. The thirsty labourers came and quenched their thirst and gave flowers to him in return. Sundar took the flowers to the same temple on the hillock and sold them. Many days passed in this manner. Now the labourers had become very friendly with Sundar. Though they were giving him flowers everyday in return, they were not satisfied. The labourers used to tell Sundar that simply giving flowers in return for Sattu was not enough and that they would be happy if they could do something more for him. But Sundar would always tell them that he would let them know when the time came.

Though Sundar was able to earn some money everyday, he was not satisfied. He wanted to earn more, so that he could send some money to his old parents.

One evening, while returning after selling flowers, he was contemplating ways of enhancing his income.

Suddenly black clouds gathered all around in the sky. There was a great storm and it began raining cats and dogs.

The inn was not very far. First Sundar thought of taking shelter in some nearby house or shop; but, then he thought that the rain might continue throughout the night; so, it would be better to go straight to the inn.

And thus, without caring for the storm and the heavy rains, he continued moving undeterred. He reached the inn safely, put his pitcher and basket in a corner, changed his dress, took meals and finally went to sleep. The storm was getting more and more violent; the clouds were thundering so loud that the claps of thunder shook the houses in the town.

Next day when he woke up in the morning, the owner of the inn gave a description of the havoc the storm had caused last night. He said that many buildings had been razed to the ground and many trees on the royal road and in the forest had been uprooted. But now the weather had become clear.

It had become so cold that Sundar considered it uselesss to go and sell cold Sattu in such bad weather. But still he set out towards the garden to meet the gardeners. In order to reach the garden he had to pass through a small forest. While passing through the forest, he saw many big trees uprooted and lying on the ground. He stopped and began thinking—'Under every circumstances, if there is a loss, there has to be a gain also. If the storm has demonstrated its negative aspects, it must be having its positivities as well. But what that positive aspect is? What profits could be earned from this kind of situation? If a dead mouse could yield some money, these fallen trees also could. And suddenly an idea flashed across his mind—'Oh, what a late realisation?'—mumbling these words he ran straight towards the garden. Within moments he was standing before the chief of the gardeners and talking to him—"Uncle! You had said once that all of you wanted to do something for me. So uncle, the time has come now."

"Yes, yes, my son! Tell us—What is it that you want us to do for you?" said the chief of the gardeners.

"Look, uncle! I did not bring Sattu today due to cold weather. But still I wanted to meet you all. While coming to this garden I saw a number of trees uprooted by the storm. I hit upon an idea that I should cut the logs into small pieces and sell them in the market."

"That's great, my son! It's a very good idea. What kind of help do you suggest that we should render?"

"Uncle, I need an axe and some bullock-carts. I shall have the logs cut into small pieces by evening and then all of you will please carry it to the market for me in your bullock-carts."

"Why not, my son, why not!" said all the gardeners in unison. "You have done so much for us. Can't we do even so little for you?"

"But my son---!" said the chief of the gardeners, "It will not be easy for you to cut the logs all alone. You please wait for some time. We shall dispose of our work and then accompany you to the forest. All of us will help you in cutting the logs and loading them on our bullock-carts. Once it is loaded you can take it wherever you want.

And then the gardeners did exactly as they had promised. They disposed of their work as fast as they could and went to the forest with Sundar with their axes. It was beyond imagination for Sundar to see them working for him so enthusiastically. They cut the logs and loaded all their bullock-carts.

After the bullock-carts were fully loaded, Sundar took them to the market.

Firewood traders used to come in the market. They used to buy firewood from there and sell them in the far-off villages. The firewood that Sundar had brought were neatly cut. So the traders became very happy and bought all his firewood without any higgling or delay.

Sundar made a good earning from the firewood. this was very encouraging for him. Now it had become clear to him that with the help of courage and wisdom, even the impossible could be made possible.

Having sold all his firewood, Sundar went straight to the owner of the inn, who had developed a fatherly affection for him. The old man became very happy when Sundar explained everything to him.

"Bravo, my son! You have done a miracle in this town. Indeed this country needs wise and intelligent young boys like you. It is young boys like you who bring name and fame to their parents and the country.

"It is all the miracle of the dead mouse, uncle!" said Sundar with a smile.

"Now my son! I have only one desire, and that is—you should progress day and night. But always remember one thing..."

"What is it uncle?"

"First thing is that you should never fall pray to egotism and second thing is that you should never oppress the poor. Every egotist has to face humiliation one day, and, my son, a poor man's cry can bring anyone to a ruin. Always try to do good to others.

"I shall always remember this, uncle!" said Sundar.

"Oh, yes! I forgot to tell you one thing," said the old man.

"What is it, uncle?"

"Look, my son! If you want, you can become rich overnight."

"Uncle, what kind of job is it? I myself wish to become rich overnight and get my parents out of poverty."

"Son, a trader of horses is coming to this town day after tomorrow with five hundred horses."

"Now you need not tell me anything; I have understood everything." Sundar had a sharp brain. He grasped it immediately.

"What did you understand, my son?"

"Since hundreds of horses are being brought to this town, they would be needing fodder also."

"Yes, my son! this is what I meant. You arrange fodder for the horses and I am sure you will make a good earning.

"You are right, uncle! I shall start making arrangements from tomorrow."

"But, my son! how will you arrange grass and fodder in such huge quantities?"

"Uncle, I know I can do it. I shall make all the arrangements."

"All right, my son! May God help you! Now you go to your room, get fresh and I shall send something for you to eat."

Sundar was greatly relieved. He took his meals and slept without any worries in his mind. Next day he went straight to a confectioner's shop. He had already made his plans to arrange grass and fodder for horses.

He said to the confectioner—"Sir, kindly arrange a basketful of Laddoos for me."

"Right away, brother!" said the confectioner.

The confectioner immediately got a basketful of Laddoos packed and handed it over to Sundar. Sundar picked up the basket of Laddoos and went straight to the garden.

The gardeners and labourers had already seen Sundar from a distance. They ran towards him. All of them were curious to know about the fate of the firewood that Sundar had taken to the market.

"O brother Sundar! Where is your pitcher in which you used to bring Sattu for us?"

"Dear brothers, instead of Sattu I have brought Laddoos for you. Come on, have your fill; eat as many as you like." And Sundar began distributing Laddoos among them.

"Oh, my son!" said the chief of the gardeners. "What is the occasion? Why are you distributing Laddoos among us?"

"Uncle, I got good money for the firewood that I had taken to the market for sale with the kind help of all of you. So I decided to celebrate the occasion by distributing sweets among you all."

"My son, you deserve praise for the love and affection that you have for the poor; especially when there is selfishness all around. Look, my son! we shall be only too pleased to know if there is anything that we can do for you."

"Yes, uncle! there is one thing you can do for me."

"Yes, yes, tell us."

"Tell us, brother Sundar," said all the labourers enthusiastically. "We shall be extremely happy to do anything for you."

"I need five hundred sackloads of fresh grass."

"When do you need it my son?" asked the chief.

"By tomorrow morning."

"This is no problem; all of us, after finishing our job, shall start cutting grass for you; but, the problem with us is that we don't have sacks. Do one thing—go to the market, arrange the sacks, and in the meanwhile, we shall have finished our job."

"All right, uncle!"

And in a very short time Sundar arranged five hundred sacks and

handed them over to the gardeners.

Next day the gardeners had five hundred sackloads of grass ready. Sundar got the sackloads of grass loaded on bullock-carts and brought them to the open field where the traders were supposed to encamp.

Sundar got a tent pitched for himself in the same field. The money that he had earned from the sale of firewood, turned out to be a great source of relief for him. And above all the labourers were helping him, which in itself was invaluable. There is great force and power in love and affection. Sundar was getting so much co-operation from their side for the sympathy he had sown to them that he was simply overwhelmed.

×　　　　　　×　　　　　　×

Next day!

The trader of the horses arrived there early in the morning. A moment ago there was complete peace and silence in the field, and now there was a din of neighing hungry horses all around. The owner of the horses was worried about the arrangement of grass and fodder for his horses. The total quantity of fodder that he had taken with himself before starting his journey, had exhausted during his transit period.

The servants had started fastening the horses in the pen when, in order to take advantage of the situation, Sundar came to the trader of horses.

"Namaste Sir! I am Sundar. I welcome you in our state. Please do let me know, if there is anything that I could do for you."

"Dear son, right now I need grass for my horses. Could you arrange good quality grass for my horses? See my horses are starving."

"Sir, you have come to our state; you are our guest, and extending hospitality to our guests is our duty. As soon as I learnt that you are coming, I started making arrangements. And now the position is that there is ample quantity of grass available for your horses. Please send your servants with me.

And thus, the problem was solved and the trader became very happy. He said, "Well done, my son! you have solved my problem. Here it is; one hundred gold coins for you."

Sundar became very happy to see hundred gold coins. Sundar had become a rich man overnight.

Once again Sundar remembered and thanked the dead mouse about which the treasurer of the king had made a mention, and had said that using one's wit and wisdom one could earn some money out of a dead mouse also. And what to talk of 'some money', he had become quite a rich man with the help of the dead mouse now.

Holding the bag of gold coins carefully, Sundar returned to the inn quickly.

Sundar was very happy and was thinking that the time had come when he was in a position to make all his dreams come true.

He began planning to bring his parents also to the town, so that, at least now, they could pass the remaining span of their life peacefully and comfortably.

The owner of the inn saw that Sundar was very happy and his face was gleaming with happiness. He said, "How was the day today? And where were you last night?

Sudar explained to him everything in detail, and told him how he had earned hundred gold coins by selling sackloads of grass to the trader.

"Uncle! Now I have hundred gold coins in my possession, and this is all with your blessings. I shall be very happy if you kindly give me one or two more such tips and help me earn some more money, so that I could bring my parents to the town and make them happy. I want them to see how their son has progressed and risen to this status."

"My son, I have got yet another tip", said the owner of the inn. "If you correctly use your wisdom, you will be able to earn even more than what you have earned."

"You have got yet another tip? Uncle, please tell me," said Sundar excitedly. "I shall follow all your advices; I shall do everything you tell me."

"My son, last night two men from some other state had come and stayed in my inn. They were saying that a big group of cloth-merchants is going to come to our capital next month. They sell their cloths to wholesalers and the wholesalers sell them to retailers. If you act on my advice, I am sure, you will earn a lot of money."

"And what shall I have to do?" asked Sundar enthusiastically.

And the old man began whispering his plans in his ear.

Sundar was overjoyed to hear his plan and said, "You are great, uncle! Now you need not worry. I shall arrange everything in such a manner that there will be nothing but success. I shall have your inn remodelled completely. There will be no inn in this town as commodious and so full of facilities, as of yours."

"My son, by divine grace, I am happy with whatever little I have. I always pray to God that every young man of this state should prosper and become happy."

Sundar remained sitting with the old man—the owner of the inn— for a long time, and discussed all the ins and outs of the business that he was going to get into, in the next month.

After a few days Sundar, at the advices of the old man, rented a house near the inn and sent a letter to his parents informing them of his success and also telling them that he would be paying a visit very soon.

Meanwhile, he opened a small cloth-shop in his house and his good reputation brought him success in this line also gradually.

The old man was also of great help to him. He had advised all his near and dear ones to buy cloths from Sundar's shop only.

But despite all this success Sundar had remained as humble as ever. All he had was a pair of clothes and a little money given by his parents when he came to this town. He had never forgotten this.

But now, with his hard work and sincerity, he had achieved great success. Now he was no more the same 'Sundar', people had begun calling him Sundar Lal Ji.

Sundar had not forgotten the labourers and gardeners—his friends—for whom he used to carry Sattu everyday.

Even now he used to spare some time for them out of his busy time.

Gradually one month passed and he had chalked out his plans to make very good profits from the cloth merchant .

One day, the old man reminded him and said, "Sundar, I am sure you remember that the cloth merchants are arriving tomorrow."

"Yes, uncle! I remember; I very well remember, and I have got my own plans to make a very good earning from them. You will see that the biggest cloth merchant will be your Sundar only in this town."

"I am happy to hear that, my son! What is your plan?"

"Uncle, you had advised me to buy the cloths from the cloth merchants and sell it to the merchants of the town in order to make a good profit. Hadn't you?"

"Yes! But I had also told you that you will be needing a lot of money for getting into this trade. Have you arranged some money?"

"My wit is my wealth, uncle! and I shall show such miracles of my wits that all the merchants of the town will be simply wonderstruck."

And then Sundar explained to him his plans.

Next day, before sunrise, a big group of merchants arrived on the bank of the river, with a lot of merchandise.

The merchants began unloading their bundles of cloth one by one from their boats and putting them on the bank of the river. Some servants began pitching tents for their masters—the cloth merchants.

Sundar was fully prepared. He also had his tent pitched with guy ropes and a horse-cart standing before it.

The chief of the visiting cloth merchants was Seth Ganga Prasad.

"Sundar," said the old man in a whispering tone.

"Yes, uncle!"

"Come on! Let's start our work now," the old man said. "The merchants have taken rest and now they are about to start selling their merchandise."

"All right, uncle! I am going to get ready now." Saying this, Sundar began changing his clothes.

The old man had already arranged Rajasthani garments and a horse-cart for him one day earlier.

Now, after being fully dressed, Sundar looked exactly like a Marwari trader. And the old man disguisd himself as his accountant.

When Sundar and the old man arrived on the bank of the river, all the cloth merchants began looking at them with surprise.

The chief of the merchants was telling his fellow merchants— "Brothers! He is a new face in this town. We had never seen him before."

"Yes, chief! what you say is correct. See, his accountant is coming towards us."

"Namaste Seth Ji," said the old man.

"Namaste, Namaste," said the visiting cloth merchants.

"Sir," the old man began talking to the chief of the cloth merchants— "Our Seth Sundar Lal Ji, who is from Jodhpur, wishes to enter into trade with you—you must have heard the name of our seth—he is a very big cloth merchant."

"Yes, yes, I have heard his name." And then the chief said, "Now please tell us what he wants from us."

"Brother, Seth Sundar Lal Ji wants all of you to sell all your merchandise to him only. He will buy your merchandise at the cost fixed by you. Money is no consideration."

"Sir, if your Seth Sundar Lal Ji is ready to buy our merchandise at the costs fixed by us, there cannot be any reason why we would not sell our goods to him," said the chief and then turning towards his fellow merchants, he said, "Why brothers...?"

"Yes, yes, we have no objection," said all the fellow merchants in unison.

"But there is a precondition, sir," said the old man.

"What is it?"

The payment will be made four days later. Meanwhile, you please accept the hospitality of Seth Sundar Lal Ji, and be comfortable."

"All right! you please bring your Seth Ji to our place; we shall have everything on paper." Then the chief turned towards his follow merchants and said, "Why friends? Wouldn't this save us from going through all the rigmaroles of selling our merchandise to so many different merchants and higgling with them as well?"

"Do as you deem fit, sir," said all the fellow merchants.

And thus, the old man and Sundar took all the merchandise of the merchants in their possession.

And within no time, on the bank of the river, a canopy was pitched with a board hanging outside, displaying the name of Seth Sundar Lal Ji, cloth Merchant from Jodhpur.

The other wholesale traders of the town came after some time and were greatly astounded to see a board, bearing name—Seth Sundar Lal Ji. "Where has this new trader come from?" they began asking each other. And then they went to the chief of the cloth merchants, and after greeting each other they asked, "Seth Ji! what merchandise have you brought this time?"

"Brothers! we had brought very good cloths, but this time Seth Sundar Lal Ji bought all our merchandise.

"What did you say? He has bought all your merchandise?" All the wholesalers began looking at the chief of the merchants with surprise.

"Yes, yes, brothers! Seth Sundar Lal Ji is a big businessman. We have earned a good profit from him," said the fellow merchants.

"But what shall we do now? Since we depended solely upon you, we did not trade with other merchants."

"O dear Dhaniram Ji! Why do you feel bothered? Now instead of trading with us, you can trade with Seth Sundar Lal Ji."

"But sir, it's a matter of shame that you have ignored your old customers and sold your merchandise to a new trader," said the wholesalers.

"Look brothers! Shame has no place in the line of trading. Money and wisdom are two aspects of business. Sundar Lal used his intelligence and bought all our merchandise before anyone of you could even reach this place. Moreover, he has given us good profits also. 'First come, first serve' is the main motto of business. Dear brothers! It's still not too late. Go and trade with Sundar Lal Ji now. Please don't waste your time here; or else, you will be deprived of whatever little you can get, if he moves out of this town and sells his merchandise in some other town."

"Yes, what you say is correct", said the wholesalers with a lost lustre of countenance.

And then, all the wholesalers went together to the tent of Seth Sundar Lal Ji. And Sundar sold all the merchandise to them at a margin of profit of twenty percent. In trying to compete with other wholesalers, every wholesaler bought as much as he could, as none wanted the other to earn more profits than him.

The owner of the inn, who was, at present, in the disguise of Sundar's accountant, was greatly surprised to see Sundar's deftness in dealing with the wholesalers. By evening all his merchandise had been sold. He calculated the shares of the visiting cloth merchants and made payments to them at their rates.

He had earned more than one lakh rupees in this business. Now he had really become Seth Sundar Lal Ji.

Thinking that Seth Sundar Lal Ji was a boy of very young age, the chief of the wholesalers said, "Sundar Lal Ji, how is it that you are handling business at such a large scale at such a young age? Your father and grandfather must have been great businessmen of their times.

"Brother Dhaniram Ji! Generally what happens—when someone has earned a little, he forgets his past and comes out with inflated ego. But I am not one of those; I am a son of a poor labourer. I came to this town a few months ago. And there was a time when I was almost on the verge of starvation and had hardly any clothes to wear. But I am greatly thankful to the treasurer of the king and also the dead mouse who helped me become a rich man."

"I did not quite get it, sir—treasurer...dead mouse?"

"Yes, brother!" And then Sundar narrated his story to Seth Dhaniram.

"You are great Sundar Lal Ji! You have no parallel," said Seth Dhaniram. "If all the young boys of this country work hard and apply their wisdom like you, their is no doubt that there will be no end to prosperity in this country.

And thus, yesterday's 'Sundar' had become 'Seth Sundar Lal' of today. He got the inn of the old man completely remodelled. He arranged many kinds of facilities in that inn; facilities that were not even thought of in those days. He brought his parents also to the town. His parents became very happy to see his prosperity. They were very thankful to God that He had given them a virtuous son. His mother used to say again and again—'O God! I wish everyone had a son like my son.

❑ ❑

2

REAL DISCIPLE

Pᴀɴᴅɪᴛ Ramnarain was the greatest scholar of his time. He was respected by all.

He had his Ashram* in a jungle outside Kanchanpur. Students from far-off places came to him to get education.

Panditji never observed any difference among his students. Be it son of a king or that of a beggar; everyone was imparted education without any discrimination.

Panditji had a daughter. She was his only issue, and was moving towards adolescence very fast. Panditji wanted to get her married as soon as possible and fulfil his duty.

His daughter was very affable, gentle and wise.

Panditji was looking for a just as affable, gentle and wise boy for her.

One day, an idea of putting all his disciples to test, flashed across the mind of Panditji. He decided that he will give his daughter's hand in marriage to the most suitable one.

Next day Panditji called all his disciples and said, "My children! I am in a very difficult situation."

"What kind of difficult situation is it, sir," asked a young boy whose name was Bhimsen.

"In fact, my daughter has become marriageable, and I have never saved anything for this purpose. Now I have decided to get her married at an early date and I shall be needing clothes and ornaments for her."

"There isn't anything to be worried about," said a handsome young boy. "You only have to wish and I shall offer thousands of gold coins at your feet. My father is the wealthiest person of the town.

"No, no, sir! I shall feel greatly obliged if I am given a chance. I am

*hermitage

the prince of this kingdom. Just make a hint and I shall bring heaps of diamonds, pearls, gold and silver at your feet.

Thus, many young boys came forward with their offers according to their capability.

But Panditji did not accept anyone's offer and said, "No, no, I shall have lost my prestige in this manner. People will say that Panditji has stooped to begging to get his daughter married."

"In that case, sir, you please suggest some way yourself. Tell us, in what way we can solve your problem," Prince Veersingh said.

"My children! you have to do something that may serve my purpuse without jeopardizing my status of a Guru. So, I suggest to you all to commit thefts and bring the required things little by little; but remember one thing—no one should know about it; if your right hand is involved in thievery, your left hand should not know about it. It should be a top secret."

"Please do not worry, sir!" said all the disciples in unison. "Your orders will be carried out."

And then the group of the disciples dispersed in all directions in order to carry out the orders of their Guru.

Whichever disciple brought clothes or ornaments, quietly handed it over to Guruji.

In a few days, Guruji had lots of clothes and ornaments accumulated in his Ashram.

Guruji was carefully keeping thing's separately, brought by each of his disciples.

After a few days, Guruji noticed that almost every disciple except Bhimsen had brought something or the other. Bhimsen had not yet stolen anything for Guruji.

So, one day, Guruji gathered all his disciples and said, "Bhimsen, every disciple of mine has stolen something for me according to his capability, but so many days have passed, and I find that you have not stolen anything for me. Is it that you don't want to help me reduce my stress and worry?"

"I do want to reduce your stress and worry, Gurudev," said Bhimsen humbly.

"Then why is it that you did not steal anything for me?"

"How could I do that, Gurudev? Your orders were such that it always checked me from doing so," said Bhimsen.

"What do you mean?" Pandit Ramnarain looked at him with sharp eyes.

The other disciples were dumbfounded. Guruji had himself asked us to commit thefts; then what kind of orders was he talking about?

"Guruji!" Bhimsen said, "You had yourself instructed us to commit thefts, but it was with a precondition that no one should know about it. Even if our right hand was involved in thievery, our left hand should not know about it.

"Yes, I had said that, but what was the problem?"

"Guruji! You have yourself taught us that there isn't anything that is hidden from our souls. In that case, how could I have kept a secret of it from my soul? This is the only reason why I could not steal anything till today."

"You are great, my son!" Pandit Ramnarain patted his back and praised him. He embraced him and said, "Bhimsen! You are my real disciple." Then turning towards other disciples, he said, "Look, my children! I am very happy that all of you are very obedient and you have obeyed me, taking all sorts of risks; but, my children! remember one thing—if your parents, your brothers and sisters or even if your Guru asks you to do something wrong, you should refuse to do it. Never do anything wrong in your life. I had staged this scene to put you all to test and also to find a suitable boy for my daughter's marriage. And now I am proud to declare that Bhimsen is the most suitable boy for my daughter."

"I am sure you must have learnt a new lesson. Now all of you please go and return all the things that you have stolen, to their owners."

"Guruji, we admit that Bhimsen is the worthiest of all of us. We accept him as the son-in-law of our Guru." Saying this all the disciples lifted Bhimsen on their shoulders and began dancing merrily.

❏ ❏

3

GRAVES AND GRAVES

AWAY from the town, nestled in the lap of hills, there was a small village—Akrampur.

Majority of the residents in that village was of labourers working in farms. And one of them was a farmer who was known as Rahim uncle.

Rahim had a wife—Farida—and one son—Karim—in his family.

Rahim worked day and night to bring up Karim suitably. He had a very small piece of land. His oxen also were weak and old. Worst of all, a major portion of his small piece of land was full of stones and was barren.

Karim had reached the age of fifteen or sixteen, but Rahim never allowed him to go towards the field. He only wanted that his son should eat, play and enjoy his life. There should not be the slightest of problem in his life. According to him, Rahim was still a small child. Sometimes Karim's mother would say—

"Karim's father! why do you keep expending yourself in the field day and night—how long will you continue to pester yourself? By God's grace, our son is grown up now. Why don't you take him to the field with yourself and make him share your burden? Everyday I see him whiling away his time with his friends after returning from school."

"Oh, mother of Karim! After all, what is his age that I should make him work in the field?" Rahim would say—"At this age he should be allowed to enjoy his life. Have you forgotten how fervently we had prayed for an issue, when we didn't have one? And now since God was kind enough to listen to our prayers and blessed us with a son, isn't it our duty to impart proper education to him, so that he becomes a big man one day? What is there in farming? I wish to make him a big officer, not a farmer."

"Yes, yes, even if you die of hard work. Look at your body and see how weak you have become. You are nothing more than a simple skeleton; you have become old before age."

"O darling! Please do not worry about me. What if I am getting old? I am happy my son is growing into a healthy and handsome youth; and this is sufficient for me," said Rahim with pride. "Do not worry. We shall have a comfortable life, when our son becomes an officer—our son will take care of us till the end of our life."

"You and your imaginations! Are the children dependable these days? Who knows whether he will give us even a square meal in future? Someone has correctly said—'If it comes to that, a father can take care of a hundred children; but even one hundred children together cannot take care of one single father.'

"You have gone mad, darling!" said Rahim looking at his wife with surprise. "What kind of mother are you that you don't even trust your own son!"

"Look dear! first I am a wife and then a mother. A woman's life and happiness is restricted to her husband's existence only. Who cares for a widow? A time comes when a widow becomes a burden on her children also."

"All right! Now please let us stop this conversation," said Rahim lifting his hand. "You may say anything, but I have full faith in my Karim—it's funny, you don't understand even this much."

"I understand everything; it is you who is not able to get the point. You don't understand the bitter truths of the world."

"And what is that bitter truth?" asked Rahim without changing his countenance.

"What I mean to say is that so long as you do not become physically infirm, your son will take full care of you; he will flatter you, but after you become weak, you will become a burden on him."

"This will never happen darling, never! The Almighly cannot be so cruel that a son, who is being taken care of by me with my blood and sweat, will, one day, turn his eyes on me and become hostile." If Rahim was right, Farida too was right. But none of the two knew what the future had in its womb for them.

Time never stops.

Time kept rolling on in this kind of sweet arguments between the husband and wife. Rahim continued with working hard in order to be able to arrange everything that might be necessary for taking care of his son.

Karim had now grown up into a handsome youth. Rahim got him married to a beautiful girl. That day Rahim was feeling extremely happy to see his son dressed as a bridegroom. Farida too was very happy.

Their days were passing in complete merriment when the village—Akrampur was hit by plague in epidemic form. Karim's mother fell prey to it and died. This brought such a profound shock on Rahim that he almost went mad. Karim and his wife were also sad; they too wept bitterly, but it was momentary. But Rahim had become almost a living corpse. Now he was not able to do hard work. Gradually he became bedridden and the job of farming came on the shoulders of Karim.

Karim was as gentle and laborious as Rahim had wanted him to become, but his wife was very clever and selfish.

Gradually a little more time passed and Jameela gave birth to a beautiful male child. Rahim named him—Iqbal—with great love and affection.

Rahim, Karim and Jameela's world had changed. Iqbal had become a great source of happiness to all of them. Rahim used to feel very happy when Iqbal lisped and called him grandfather. Rahim used to pass all his time around Iqbal. Iqbal also could not live without him even for a second. From morning till evening they used to be together. At night Rahim would call from his room—'Karim, my son! come and take Iqbal to his mother; he is asleep.'

Such was the love between the grandfather and the grandson.

But as Iqbal was growing, Rahim's health was going down. God knows what disease he had caught that he would keep coughing throughout the day lying in his room. Old age and disease together brought gradual deterioration in his health. Old age in itself is worse than hundreds of diseases.

In the beginning Karim took full care of his ailing father. He consulted the best available doctors of his village. But now Karim had begun feeling a little frustrated. And Jameela—being altogether different in nature—felt more frustrated.

One day Karim said to his wife, "Jameela, I think I should take my father to town and consult the best available doctor there in some good hospital.

"Have you gone mad, Karim Miyan?" said an enraged Jameela. "What's left in your father now that you are planning to waste your money on him? If not today, he is going to die tomorrow. If you at all wish to exercise your brain, think of Iqbal. Our future lies in Iqbal, not in your father. What will you achieve by wasting your money on your already dying father?

Karim had no vices; he was simple and gentle, but his greatest drawback was that he was henpecked. He had no idea of the worldly affairs. Earlier he had been obeying his parents and now he was obeying his wife.

Jameela's continuous goading brought some change in him. Now he wasn't as sincere as he used to be towards his father. The only thing he did was earning and giving all his earning to his wife everyday.

Jameela would spend at her whim and Karim never took an account of her expenditure.

Iqbal was growing gradually. He used to spend most of the day with his grandfather. The truth was that it was only Iqbal who shared his grandfather's grief and pain. Karim, to some extent, cared for his father and enquired about his health in the morning and evening, but Jameela would not even enter his room. Whenever Jameela heard Rahim coughing, she would pray to God to put an end to his life.

One day, in utter disgust, she said to Rahim, "Look, I am really fed up with the illness of your father; he keeps coughing day and night; I am afraid, he is suffering from some contagious disease, and it's not safe for the health of our son—Iqbal. For the whole day Iqbal is moving around this old man. What shall we do if he too catches some disease?"

"What you say is correct, Jameela," said Karim in a sad tone. "But you yourself suggest to me if there is any remedy. Iqbal also cannot live without him."

"Think about your son," she said, "I would suggest to you that you should get rid of this problem as early as possible."

"How to get rid of the problem? Do you mean to say that I should strangle him?"

"No, no, don't strangle him; just throw him into some river or pond in the darkness of the night. Thus, your father will get rid of his problems and we too shall be in peace."

"But imagine what people will say."

"Do you think you will be taking him out with orchestra along with you. Just dump him in your bullock-cart and take him away when it is dark. If our neighbours and kiths and kins enquire about him, I shall tell them that you have taken your father to town for a better treatment. All

that you have to do is to push him into the river while crossing the bridge. Don't think you are killing him; you should think that you are freeing him from all sorts of problems of illness. Later I shall tell everyone that the old man died in the town and my husband cremated him there only."

"No, no," Rahim was shocked to hear the formidable plans of his wife, "I cannot do this; such things can never remain a secret. Our relatives will tear us into pieces when they come to know about it."

"If you cannot do even this much, you better stay with this living corpse; I am going to my parent's house."

"No, no, Jameela! Don't do that. What shall become of me? What will happen to Iqbal?

"How do I know what will happen? If you at all wish to keep me with yourself, you shall have to get rid of this living corpse." Then suddenly she spoke in a decisive tone—"Tell me! You are going to keep him in the house or...?"

"No, no, Jameela! you stay here; but please think over it again. Killing one's father..."

"O God! why the hell are you adamant on proving a dead man a living being? All right! you do one thing—you need not go too far. There is a jungle behind our village. Take him there, dig a grave and bury him quietly. Neither there will be much row, nor will anyone come to know about it. Rest I shall take care of."

Karim was helpless. He was being torn between father and wife. Ultimately, Karim gave in. He thought—'My father has to die some day or the other, whereas I have to pass my life with my wife. So it is more practical to do what she says.' He knew killing one's father is a great sin, but if Jameela left him and went away, Iqbal's life would be ruined.'

At last he decided to do what Jameela wanted.

One day!

Karim took out his bullock-cart, when it was past mid-night.

It was the black night of Amavasya*. Darkness and desolation

*The last day of the dark half of a month.

loomed large at night. The whole village was sleeping comfortably. Old Rahim was also lying half unconscious in his bed. He was breathing with difficulty. With every breath of his, came a strange sound as if his throat was choking. This kind of sound produced by his throat made the night all the more frightening.

Jameela and Kareem were standing near his bed.

"Now what are you waiting for? Take the old man together with his cot, dump him in your bullock-cart and take him away from here quietly. I have already put a shovel and other things in your bullock-cart, that you may require while digging."

"Jameela!" said Karim almost in tears. "My heart does not allow me to do this. Just think how heinous a crime it is? What big sin you are forcing me to commit?"

"Don't behave like a mad man! Do as I say. "Then threatening him, she said, "Now if you don't listen to me, I shall start shouting and gather the villagers here. Ultimately the result will be that you will be trapped. I shall tell them that in utter frustration of your father's prolonged illness, you were taking him to jungle to bury him alive. I am a woman; everyone will believe me and you will be incarcerated."

Jameela's threatening worked. He was terribly frightened.

He began perspiring profusely at the name of imprisonment, and began trembling with fear.

"Come on! pick up the cot," said Jameela holding the cot at one end.

In utter compulsion he had to help Jameela lift the cot, and within moments the cot was dumped into the bullock-cart along with old Rahim.

Though they were doing all this very quietly, without making any noise, God knows how Iqbal got the clack of foot steps and woke up. Finding none in the room, seven year old Iqbal began calling his mother and came out of his room. Seeing the ghastly scene outside his room, he stopped weeping, and asked in utter dismay—"Ammi! Abbu! what are you doing here? Oh, God! this is my grandfather lying in the bullock-cart. Where are you taking my grandfather?"

Karim's heart began pounding abnormally, but Jameela somehow managed to maintain her cool and said, "My son! Your father is taking your grandfather to town for treatment."

"In that case I too shall accompany him. I shall nurse him there."

"No, no, my son!" said Kairm with nervousness. "I shall be there to nurse him."

"If you will stay with my grandfather for nursing him, who will earn money to buy medicines for my grandfather? No, no, I shall definitely accompany my grandfather."

"But, my son! You are still too young. Where will you stay in the town?"

"I shall stay with my grandfather."

"But, my son! your grandfather is going to be hospitalised," said Karim feeling a bit annoyed.

"I shall also remain in the hospital with my grandfather."

"Look, Iqbal! My son! Don't insist..."

"I don't want to hear anything. I will definitely go with my grandfather."

Both husband and wife were nonplussed. They didn't know how to manage the situation. They were terribly scared. Thinking that if Iqbal began weeping, they wouldn't succeed in their plans. His weeping may wake up their neighbours; and if the neighbours began enquiring, they shall have no reply. Now ultimately fulfilling the demand of Iqbal was the only alternative.

Meanwhile, Iqbal got into the bullock-cart and began watching his grandfather's face carefully.

"What shall we do now, Jameela? I think, we should change our decision."

"You have gone mad! You only know how to spoil a game. Now listen..." And Jameela began to whisper something in his ear.

Karim only kept nodding like fools.

And then!

After some time Karim and Iqbal had set out in their bullock-cart, and the bullock-cart was moving slowly on the uneven road.

It was eerily slilent all around.

What could be heard were the jingling of bells of the oxen and creaking sound of wheels.

The bullock-cart kept moving for long. Since young Iqbal was already feeling sleepy, he put his head on the chest of his grandfather and fell asleep.

Leaving the footpath, the bullock-cart had now entered the dense forest.

Karim parked his bullock-cart in the shelter of a tree, and taking out his shovel very quietly, he went behind bushes and began digging.

Only a few moments had passed, when Iqbal opened his eyes and began looking around. There was none around. A child is after all a child, and so was Iqbal. He almost began getting paralysed with fright. Suddenly, he heard sounds of shovel digging the earth. Now he was terribly frightened. He looked around; his father—Karim was also not there.

"Abbu! Abbu!"

He called out Karim many times, but he was only responded by eeriness and the sounds of shovel digging the earth.

"Where has Abbu gone?" Iqbal jumped out of the bullock-cart and began moving towards the direction from which the sound of digging of earth was coming. The dreadful surronding was making him jittery.

"Oh, God!" Despite the darkness of night he could clearly distinguish that it was his father—Karim. "Abbu! what on earth are you doing here?"

Karim was busy digging grave for his father. He was startled to hear Iqbal calling him—"Iqbal! you?"

"Abbu! Abbu! Why are you digging this pit?"

Iqbal could not think of a suitable reply. He said with nervousness—"Why have you come here, my son? Go and sit with your grandfather."

"No, first you tell me the reason why you are digging a pit here."

"Look, Iqbal!" Karim became angry this time. "You are becoming too obstinate day by day. Go, sit with your grandfather and let me do my

work."....."obstinate child of an obstinate mother," he mumbled to himself. "I don't know what made me listen to Jameela...and now I am in this trouble."

"Abbu! Listen!" Iqbal was getting more and more curious. "I shall not budge an inch from here, until you tell me the reason why you are digging this pit; rather, I shall start weeping and wake up my grandfather also."

Karim was terribly frightened to hear this. There were beads of perspiration on his upper lip due to nervousness. "No, no, don't do this," he said in a mild tone.

There will be hell of a lot of trouble, if he starts weeping. Thinking this, Karim came near him, and fondling him with love, he said, "Look, my son! I am doing all this to bring peace to your grandfather's soul."

"What...I have heard that this is done for the dead, but my grandfather is very much alive."

"He is of course alive, my son; but he is worse than a dead man. He is almost a living corpse. Don't you realise the amount of suffering that he is undergoing because of his illness. He is not going to recoup in any case and this is the only way he can rest in peace."

Iqbal was simply dumbfounded. He was young and innocent, but not so innocent so as not to be able to understand the game.

"What are you thinking, Iqbal?" As if his soul upbraided him. "Your father is going to bury your grandfather alive. Is it not enough for you to open your month?" Then, as if talking to himself, he said, "But I am too young. What can I do after all?"

Then he suggested to himself—"Tell your father that you will follow suit. You will also bury him alive in the same manner, as he is doing to his father."

And suddenly as if there was an explosion in young Iqbal's mind; as if God had given him a way out; there was certain brightness in his eyes.

"What are you thinking, Iqbal?" Karim interrupted his chain of thoughts. "Go and sit with your grandfather; and see that you don't disturb him."

"All right, Abbu!" said Iqbal. "But please give the shovel to me after you have finally finished digging the pit."

"Why, my son? What will you do with this shovel?" asked Karim in surprise. He was happy that Iqbal had finally agreed to listen to him and he wouldn't create any problems.

"Abbu! I too shall dig a pit."

"But why, my son," said Karim in great perplexity.

"Abbu! There will come a day when you too shall fall ill like my grandfather and become old; and then, I too shall bring peace to your soul in the same manner."

Iqbal's assertion came like a thunderbolt. Karim felt the earth was slipping from under his feet. He was so shocked that he could not speak. He had become speechless.

For a moment, things became entirely different. The same Iqbal began looking like a god to him. As if the god in Iqbal was telling him— 'Why are you looking at me in this manner, Karim Miyan? you will get from me exactly what you are giving your father. I am learning everything from you. As you sow, so you will reap.'

"No, no!" screamed Karim suddenly out of nervousness.

"What happened, Abbu?"

"No, no, my son, no!" Karim took him in his arms quickly. Tears welled up in his eyes. "Iqbal, my son! you have opened my eyes. I was going to commit an unpardonable crime. What a sinner I am? How selfish was it of me that I was going to kill someone who had fathered me. Come on, my son! I shall take my father to town right now, so that I can get him hospitalised for treatment and render him proper care."

And now Karim was weeping like children. "My father must have had expectations from me, like I have from you. Had he brought me up with his sweat and blood, that one day I would bury him alive. But, believe me my son, it is all because of your wretched mother. It is that wicked lady who turned me blind and filled me with selfishness. But why should I blame her. It is I who was at fault. Why did I agree to dance to her tunes despite being a man? Come on, my son! Let us go. Now I take a vow that I shall take full care of my father so long as I am alive." Karim continued with his soliloquy, unburdening his heart and mind to Iqbal and Iqbal continued looking at his father's face innocently. And then Iqbal rested his chin on his father's shoulder, and closed his eyes with a sigh of relief.

Karim's eyes had opened. He quickly picked up the shovel and returned to the bullock-cart. Karim's face was gleaming with new hopes now; as if he had a new life.

Iqbal's one single sentence—'as you sow, so you will reap'—had opened his eyes. He would definitely have faced consequences in future for what he was going to do tonight. It is rightly said that a person should think at least fifty times, before he takes a decision to do something and must always remember that every action has a reaction.

❏ ❏

4

REAL MOTHER

IN a village named Vilaspur, there were two women—Bholi and Chanchala; they were very good friends. Everyday, after their husbands had gone out to work, they would come and sit together in their courtyards, and discuss their everyday experiences and problems. They would eat together and, not only that, they would even wear garments and ornaments also of each other's choice. In short, they were so deeply engrossed in their friendly affairs that they wouldn't even care for the other women of the village. Their such deep friendship had become a cause of jealousy among the other women of the village and some of them were always, looking for a chance to cause rift between them. But by divine grace, none had yet been successful.

The elders of the village used to say—'The affection between Bholi and Chanchala is exemplary. They are one soul in two bodies. Even the real sisters wouldn't have so much of affection for each other.'

They had formed a world of their own, and were happy in each other's company in it. They always maintained absolute secrecy about themselves, and it was not possible for anyone to know anything about them.

Both were issueless and had an immense desire to have a sweet child. They prayed fervently for it.

Becoming mother is every woman's ultimate wish. Every woman wants to become a mother in due time and achieve the pride of being a perfect woman. There is no woman on earth who would want to be called a barren woman.

Once the villagers saw Bholi and Chanchala with a child. None knew whose child it was. None had seen any of the two during the period of pregnancy. Both had kept the matter of pregnancy a secret from the villagers. Bholi and Chanchala, both, gave equal affection to the child. The women of the village tried many times to enquire from them as to who was the real mother of the child, but both of them responded with a furtive smile only.

The villagers would see the child with Bholi sometimes and sometimes with Chanchala. If Chanchala would bathe the child, Bholi would lull the baby into sleep.

Thus, time kept rolling on, and the child kept growing. When the villagers could, in no way, come to know as to who the real mother was, their curiosity also came to an end.

But it is rightly said that it doesn't take long to change the circumstances. No one knows for sure when someone's views and feelings may change abruptly.

One day the villagers saw Bholi and Chanchla fighting violently with each other. The whole village was greatly surprised. Growing self-interests had sown the seeds of differences between them. A deep rift had started between Bholi and Chanchala and had marked the beginning of the end of their friendship.

Only when the matter was brought before the villagers, that they came to know the real source of the rift—it was the child's ownership that had brought their years old friendship to this end. Bholi claimed that the child belonged to her, and Chanchala was denying the fact and refusing to hand over the child to her. Chanchala claimed that the child had been mothered by her. And this was the issue that had erected a wall of hatred between them. Even the village assembly could not give any final judgement in this regard, as none in the village was a witness to the real motherhood. Things went worse, when during village assembly these two women came down to a physical fight once again. It was not something unusual in the village; but only among other women. It was beyond imagination for everyone to see Bholi and Chanchala fighting.

Both the women were screaming at the top of their voices and laying claims on the child—"This is my child; I have kept this child in my womb for nine months; I am the one who has given birth to this child."

"Look, Bholi! Don't tell a lie! this is my child; I have given birth to this child. You have not had any issue till date and that's the reason why you are claiming this child, so that people don't start calling you a barren woman."

"It is you who is a barren woman, and that's the reason why you are laying claim on my child, you sinner. I kept a secret of this fact from the villagers, only to save you from bearing the sarcastic remarks on your barrenness. I always thought that one day God will listen to you also and bestow you motherhood. But you are a barren woman, and that's the reason why you want to get the ownership of the child, by hook or by crook."

"Listen, both of you!" said the chief of the village. "You will get nothing by creating this kind of farce. First tell me how this dispute arose. Both of you were rendering equal love and care to this child, and now I see that you are at daggers drawn with each other. Come on! Tell me the truth!"

"Let me tell you, chief," said Chanchala. "Everyone in the village knows that we got married at a few days' interval only, and also that none of us could become a mother even after a lapse of a period of few years after marriage. We used to share each other's griefs and sorrows. We avoided mixing up with the women of the village; only to avoid sarcastic remarks of women on our barrenness. Why Bholi? Isn't what I am saying, true?"

"Yes, that is true, but..."

"Come on! No ifs and buts!" Chanchala interrupted her. "Let me complete my version before the chief of the village."

"But I am sure, you will start telling lies now."

"I have always been on the path of truth. Why shall I tell a lie now?"

"Bholi!" said the chief of the village, before they could enter into an argument once again. "You keep quiet and let her complete her statement. Yes, Chanchala! Now tell me what happened."

"Chief! God listened to my fervent prayers, and by His grace, I conceived. Bholi was the first one on earth with whom I shared my good news, but she, instead of becoming happy, became sad. When I asked her the reason behind her sadness, she said, "Sister, Chanchala! We got married almost at the same time. God listened to your prayers and now you are in your family way, whereas, my prayers have remained unanswered. I don't even know whether I shall become a mother or not. And worst of all, the women of the village will start calling me a barren woman and make my life a hell."

"Why do you think like that? Your prayers too will be answered one day. God willing, you too will become a mother soon. Still, you may take a promise from me that I shall not declare to anyone of my pregnancy. And if you did not conceive even after I gave birth to my child, we both will bring up the child like real mothers. You too will have the same right on my child. And unfortunately this is what happened. I gave birth to a lovely child and she was deprived of the pride of becoming a mother. We both began rearing the child with great love and care."

"This much I can understand," said the chief, "but what caused you two to fight with each other?"

"Sir, the quarrel began when I heard her telling my child to call me 'aunt'. Now you yourself tell me if this is not sufficient ground for a rift. Is there any mother on earth who would agree to be called an 'aunt'? Sir, this is the reason why I became doubtful about her integrity, thinking that she wanted to take away my child from me."

"Chief! She is telling a lie! This is my child," said Bholi in a loud voice. "I am the real mother of this child. It's she who wanted the child to call me 'aunt', and take away my child from me. It's I who had told her that so long as she did not beget a child, she could treat my child as her child. I never knew she would repay me thus." Saying this Bholi began weeping bitterly. "She is a liar, chief, she is a liar. She wants to take away my child."

The chief was totally confused. Both seemed to be speaking truth. He was not able to give his judgement in favour of any of the two. Nor was he in a position to prove who the real mother was.

"Look!" At last, after having discussed the matter thoroughly with the rest of the members of the village assembly, the chief said, "This case is extremely complicated, and it's difficult to bring a genuine solution to this problem and render a final judgement. It is beyond doubt that only one of you is the mother of this child, and that, one of you is laying false claim on this child. This is a sin and a serious crime, and one of you will have to undergo severe punishment for this. So, after detailed discussion we have decided that this matter will be taken to king's court. But still we wish to give you a chance. One who is making false claim may withdraw and admit her fault. We promise that she will not be punished. But if the matter is taken to king's court, his judgement will be final, and the one who is laying false claim on the child, will be subjected to severe punishment. Now tell me! who is the liar? Is it you, Bholi?"

"No, chief, no!" Bholi writhed in agony. "I can say in the name of God that I am the one who is the real mother of the child. I tried to be good to her. I never knew that this slut would respond in this manner."

"What's your statement, Chanchala?" asked the chief.

"Sir, I have already given my statement. This child is mine and I am his real mother. Her crocodile tears can't change the facts."

"All right! The final decision of the village assembly is that this case will be submitted before the king in his court tomorrow," said the chief of village. "And until any final judgement, the child will remain in the care of the village assembly."

"All right! This is acceptable to me," said Chanchala.

"No, no, sir! this is unjust. How will this child live without me in the night?"

"Bholi! You need not worry," said the chief. "My wife herself will take care of the child and we will see to it that he is comfortable."

"Sir, she is weeping in order to gain sympathy of the village assembly. She is a sanctimonious hypocrite," said Chanchala.

"It will be better if both of you leave this place instead of casting aspersions on each other. The case will be decided in king's court now."

Thus the argument was postponed till next day, only to be decided in king's court. Both the women returned cursing each other.

Next day the chief of village submitted the case in king's court. By now, this unique case had become a topic of debate in the nearby villages and also in other parts of the state. Thus, the court was full of curious people. Everyone was curious about the final judgement to be given by the king in this unique case.

Even the king was astonished to learn that there were two claimants of the child; and both claimed to be his mother. And also that no one in the village had the slightest inkling as to who the real mother was.

The king listened to the case carefully and was lost in deep thoughts. He too was finding himself unable to come to a definite conclusion.

"This is a very serious matter," the king said to his minister.

"Yes, My Lord! It's not an ordinary case. The problem is that the child is so young that he can't give statement. And one of these two women wants to take undue advantage of this situation. My Lord! My humble suggestion in this regard is that the case may kindly be handed over to swamy Aushadhanand Ji. He is far-sighted and is a great devotee of God. Lies won't stand before him."

"Yes, minister! I agree with you. Only the Almighty God is a witness to cases which have not been witnessed by any human being; and He, in some way or the other helps solve the case. How and when He comes can be seen by a seer only. Swamy Aushadhanand Ji is a real seer. So, This is my order that the case may be submitted before Swamy Ji tomorrow.

And thus...

Next day the king and the ministers set out to the Ashram of Swamy Aushadhanand Ji with the women and the child. They were followed by countless people who were very curious to know the ultimate result of this unique case.

In a short time the king explained the case to Swamy Ji and submitting the case before him, he said, "Swamy Ji! We have come in your shelter to get a solution to this complicated problem. Please solve this dispute and bring out the truth."

Swamy Aushadhanand Ji took the child in his lap with love and looked at his face carefully. The child was playing happily in his lap. After having had a close look at the face of the child, he raised his eyes towards those two women. Both looked sad.

Swamy Ji looked at the king and said, "I know whose son is this child."

"Whose son is he, Swamy Ji," asked the king curiously.

"I shall not name her. They themselves will come out with the truth." And then turning towards the women, Swamy Ji said, "Now tell me in the name of God—whose son is this child."

Bholi began sobbing and said, "I am the mother of this unfortunate child."

"Shut up, you swine! How dare you call my son 'unfortunate'? In fact it is you who is unfortunate, because you have not yet been able to become a mother. And now you have your eyes on my child," said Chanchala in a harsh tone.

Swamy Ji was quick to realise that those two women would come down to the level of a scuffle also if they were not quietened.

"Be quiet both of you," Swamy Ji asked them to maintain peace. He was engrossed in deep thoughts. The gathering around was waiting silently for Swamy Ji to proceed the case. The eyes of the king were also fixed upon Swamy Ji with every hope to find an amicable solution to the problem. Suddenly Swamy Ji asked, "Ladies! will the judgement given by me be acceptable to you?"

"Yes Swamy Ji!" Came a quick reply from Chanchala. "Declining your judgement is out of question. There isn't anything in the universe that you are not aware of. I am sure your judgement will be an outcome of a careful consideration of all aspects of the case and on the basis of truth."

Then Swamy Ji turned towards Bholi.

"Your judgement will be acceptable to me also Swamy Ji. I am confident of the victory of truth."

"All right!" Swamy Ji got up from his place and at a short distance from his seat, he drew a circle; I shall count upto three and as soon as I finish counting three, the lady who grabs the child first will be declared the real mother of the child."

"This is acceptable to us Swamy Ji."

Swamy Ji did as he had announced a moment ago. He put the child inside the circle.

"One," Swamy Ji began the count.

"Two,"

Now both the women were ready to grab the child.

"Three."

As soon as Swamy Ji uttered 'three', both the women pounced upon the child. And, next momet, Bholi was holding the child by his legs and Chanchala by his hands.

"Leave my child, you swine; this is my child," Bholi groaned in pain.

"The child is mine, you barren woman! Let me see how you take away the child."

Both began pulling the child towards themselves.

Being pulled thus, the child began weeping loudly. Soon the child's weeping turned into wailing due to pain. The child continued crying with pain and the women continued pulling him towards themselves; each one trying to take the child in her possession.

The people around were also feeling pity to see the child in so pitiable a condition. They were greatly surprised to see that even the wailing of the innocent child did not have any effect on those two cruel women.

"No," suddenly Bholi screamed painfully. She could take no more the wailing of the child. Leaving the child she sat on the ground and began sobbing. "Swamy Ji! I cannot bear to see the child being tortured in such a manner. Please give this child to this slut, if she says that this is her child. But please see that my child is not tortured anymore."

Chanchala quickly took the child in her arms. "What did you say, you slut? Of course this child is mine. Now you can see for yourself Swamy Ji, who the real mother of the child is. Would this slut have foregone her claim so easily, had she been the real mother? It's always the truth which comes out victorious."

Once again Swamy Aushadhanand Ji was lost in deep thoughts and once again everyone's eyes were fixed upon him. Everyone was curious about the judgement of Swamy Ji and wanted to know who the real mother was.

Chanchala was still holding the child tightly in her arms and kissing it madly; and still the child was weeping.

"Chanchala!" Suddenly Swamy Ji's placid voice resounded. "Hand over the child to Bholi; you are not the real mother of this child.

"What are you saying, Swamy Ji?" screamed Chanchala. You yourself had announced that one of us who grabs the child first will be declared the real mother of the child."

"Yes, I had said that."

"Then why are you going back on your words?"

"I am trying to do justice Chanchala—justice of truth—and the truth is that this child is not yours; this is Bholi's child."

"No, no, Swamy Ji! This is unjust."

"Keep your trap shut, you nasty woman! How can a woman be considered a mother if she doesn't possess motherly love in her heart? Had you been the real mother of this child, you would, in no case, have allowed the child to undergo such torture. But since this child is not yours and you wanted to take possession of the child at any cost, you clung to every ruse. You were guided by self motives, and a selfish person doesn't feel concerned about the well-being of others. The real mother of this child is Bholi who could not bear to see the child wailing and being tortured. And simply, in order to save the child from this kind of torture, she opted to withdraw her claim." Saying this Swamy Ji turned towards the king and said, "King! I have given my judgement; and now executing it is in your hands. Do as you wish."

The king pondered over the matter again and gave his final orders—

"The child may be taken from the possession of this wicked lady and handed over to Bholi. And for the heinous crime committed by this wicked lady, she may be put behind bars.

"No, no, My Lord! Please don't do this." Saying this Bholi took the child from Chanchala and said, "My Lord! She is my friend; please don't punish her so harshly. Though of course she has done all this guided by some ulterior motives, she is not at all bad at heart."

The king turned towards Chanchala and said, "Now, do you realise how great Bholi is? You tried to cheat her and she is begging pardon for you."

"My Lord! Please forgive me. The doctor of the village had told me that I would never be able to become a mother; and this is the reason why the sinful thoughts dominated my acts." Saying this Chanchala began weeping bitterly.

"Bholi is guileless and pious, and it is because of her that I forgive you; but remember, you will be subjected to severe punishment if you ever tried to cheat anyone in future," said the king.

"Bholi, my sister!" Chanchala fell in the feet of Bholi and weeping bitterly, she said, "I know, I have hurt your feelings, but please forgive me. I shall never do this in future."

"Don't lose heart Chanchala! Let us forget everything! The tears rolling down your cheeks are the tears of repentance. From confession flows repentance and from repentance forgiveness. Now take this child and remember that you too have just as much right over the child. Today I announce before everyone that though I have given birth to this child, Chanchala will have equal rights and she will take full care of the child like a real mother. Seeing the child happy and comfortable will keep me satisfied."

Seeing the greatness of Bholi, tears welled up in the eyes of everyone present there. The king and Swamy Aushadhanand Ji were also full of praise for her.

❏ ❏

5

SO RESOLUTE A BOY

RAMDIN was known all over Varanasi. He lived on the bank of the river Ganges with his kiths and kins. His job was to fill his leathern water-bag with river water and carry it to the houses of wealthly people.

One day poor Ramdin was going towards the populated area of the town with his water-bag when suddenly he happened to see something glittering on the ground. Ramdin picked it up and there was no end to his happiness when he realised that it was a silver coin.

"Oh, Good Lord! A silver coin early in the morning! O goddess Laxmi! It's so very kind of you."

This was a good beginning for Ramdin. He was extremely happy.

Now the problem was of the safe keeping of the coin. His hut was not at all safe because it had no doors. All he had in the name of doors was a curtain hanging by the door-frame.

"O good Lord! Where to keep this money where it remains safe. I shall spend it only on some very special occasion. But the problem is of keeping it safe till then." This was a new kind of problem before him.

Ramdin was a bachelor. He thought—'Why not keep this coin in a safe place and spend it on my marriage; or may be I should purchase cosmetics and ornaments for my wife after marriage; she will be very happy.'

So, Ramdin had finally decided the mode of expenditure, but the basic problem of keeping it safe was still there. Suddenly he hit upon an idea that the safest way to keep the money secured would be to hide the coin in the hollow of the hind wall of the old palace. Since it was an isolated place, his money's safety was guaranteed.

Thinking this Ramdin set out to the old palace. This palace was at quite a distance from the town and there was no population nearby. Ramdin reached the back portion of the palace; there was a small hollow in the hind wall. He slid a few loose bricks from around the hollow; tore a piece of cloth from his turban, wrapped his coin and after hiding the coin carefully in the hollow, he replaced the bricks and now he was fully assured of the safety of his valuable coin.

"Yes, now it is all right. My money is safe here. Neither thieves nor any kind of storm can take away my wealth."

With the one-rupee silver coin Ramdin thought that he had become a very rich man. Now Ramdin was eagerly awaiting the day when he would get married and get a chance to spend his money.

Suddenly Ramdin was reminded of Paro; the daughter of Ramu—the washer man; he loved her very much and wanted to marry her. But he didn't have the guts to talk to him for Paro's hand in marriage. He thought to himself—'why not proceed through Lala Ram—the grocer of his village?' Thinking this he immediately set out to Lala Ram's shop.

"Good morning, Lala Ji!"

"Oh, Ramdin, you? How is it that you are here so early in the morning? Are you enjoying a holiday today?"

"A person who is always busy in his kitchen, cannot think of a holiday. He cannot also think of doing some business also. There should, at least, be someone in the house to look after the kitchen."

"Yes, I agree. One has to be free from the kitchen if he wants to go out on job or do some business," said Lala Ram in an agreeable tone.

Ramdin felt encouraged and said, "Lala Ji! Do you remember you had suggested to me to get married?"

"Oh, yes, yes! I remember. Ramu has also requested me to suggest some suitable boy for his daughter. If you want I can talk to him for you."

"Lala, please arrange the marriage for me. I shall feel highly obliged."

And then Lala Ram talked to Ramu and arranged his daughter's marriage with Ramdin.

Next day the marriage was solemnized and Paro came to Ramdin's hut.

Both husband and wife began living happily. Ramdin was so lost in Paro's love that he had almost forgotten about the one-rupee silver coin. He would go out on job everyday, earn some money and hand it over to Paro.

There used to be a village fair on the bank of the river Ganges every year between mid-June and mid-July.

One day Paro put her arms around his neck and said with love— "Darling! won't you take me to the village fair?"

Hearing this, Ramdin came out of the hut. He was greatly worried. This was for the first time in life that Paro had made a demand and he had no money to fulfil it. Where to get the money from?

And suddenly there was a flash across his mind. He remembered the one-rupee coin he had hidden in the hollow of the hind wall of the old palace.

It was that coin which had given rise to the idea of marriage in his mind. And after marriage he had immersed himself totally in the love of Paro and had forgotten about the money.

He quickly went back inside the hut, lifted Paro in his hands and began dancing happily.

"Oh, darling! What are you doing? Leave me. Just a moment ago you had become so sad to hear my demand, and now you are dancing with happiness as if you have hit upon some buried treasure," Paro admonished him with love and she was a little surprised also.

"In a way you can say that I have hit upon a treasure." Saying this Ramdin narrated the whole story to her.

"O good God! With one-rupee silver coin we can buy a lot of things," said Paro happily. "Look, darling! I shall definitely buy a pair of studs for my ears."

"Yes, yes! Do buy it. Now I am going to bring that silver coin. Get ready; We shall definitely go to the village fair today."

And Ramdin left for the old palace to bring his money back.

Ramdin considered that one-rupee coin a good omen for himself, as it was because of that silver coin that he could get Paro as his wife.

For him the riches of the whole world was on one side and that one-rupee silver coin was on the other side. For Ramdin, his silver coin could, in no case, be outweighed by any amount of riches.

The pace that Ramdin set for the old palace was too fast. He was almost flying in the air.

The road on which he was running, led to the old palace through a forest.

There, on the other side, was a new palace. The king was discussing something with his ministers on the roof-top of his palace.

Suddenly he saw Ramdin running madly, perspiring all over. He was greatly surprised.

"Minister!"

"Yes, My Lord!"

"Do you see this young man running towards the forest, sweating like a bullock?"

"Yes, My Lord! I do see."

"Arrange to get hold on him and bring him to me immediately. There must be some solid reason behind it. Otherwise why else should a boy be running towards the forest in the hot summer noon? I want to know. Taking care of the well-being of my subjects is my duty."

The minister immediately ordered the soldiers and within no time a soldier was seen chasing Ramdin.

After some time the soldier brought Ramdin before the king. Ramdin was standing before the king with trepidation and with his hands folded.

"Young man! Who are you and why were you running at such fast pace towards the jungle in this hot summer noon?"

"My Lord! My name is Ramdin and my job is to carry river water to the houses of the people of my surrounding area. Right now, I was going with some very urgent and important work."

"After all what was that urgent and important work for which you ignored even the scorching heat of the mid-noon?"

"My Lord! The fact is that I have hidden my treasure in the hollow of the hind wall of the old palace. I was going to get my treasure back from there so that I could take my wife to the village fair."

"Treasure?" The king was startled to hear.

"Yes, My Lord!"

"Thousand or two thousand?"

"Not even that much, My Lord!" said Ramdin. "I have got only one silver coin in my treasure."

"What?" The king got startled once again. "Only one silver coin?"

"Yes, My Lord! that's a treasure that I have kept secured for a long time."

The king continued looking at Ramdin with great surprise. He was also feeling pity for Ramdin seeing his innocence.

Whereas Ramdin was saying—"My Lord! with that one-rupee silver coin I shall take my wife to the village fair and make her happy. My Lord! I have none except my wife in the world."

"If that is the only reason why you were running towards the forest, take one silver coin from my treasury; take your wife to the village fair and make her happy. Why take so much pains?"

"My Lord! It's so very nice of you that you are kindly giving me a one-rupee silver coin, but still I shall go to fetch that particular coin, because that coin is very auspicious to me."

"Look, Ramdin! I suggest to you to give up the idea of going to the forest in this hot summer day. You are my subject and I am your king;

and taking care of the welfare of my subjects is my duty. If you think, a one-rupee silver coin is too meagre an amount, I shall ask my treasurer to give you two silver coins."

"You are our king, My Lord! I cannot decline any offer made by you, but..."

" 'But' what?"

"Even then I shall go to the forest to get my money."

"Even if I give you one hundred gold coins?"

"Yes, My Lord! Even then."

"This young boy is strangely foolish and obstinate. An offer of one hundred gold coins even, does not deter him from his decision! After all what's so special in that particular coin?" Thinking this the king asked, "O young man! What's so special about that coin that even after an offer of one hundred gold coins you wish to stick to that one-rupee silver coin only?"

"My Lord! I have already told you that that particular coin is very auspicious to me. Had I not found that coin, I wouldn't have married also. Had I not married, I wouldn't have got a beautiful and affable wife like Paro. And that's the reason, O Lord, that that coin is extremely valuable for me."

The king thought that Ramdin was a boy of firm determination, but he would have to be put to test in order to find whether he was honest or greedy. So he said, "Ramdin! Will you go to fetch that coin even if I give you one thousand gold coins?"

"Yes, My Lord! still I would go, because I had hidden that money there with a view to spend it on my wife only. And now I shall take my wife to the village fair and fulfil her demands with that coin."

"But since I am giving you a thousand times more than the value of your hidden treasure, you should, at least now, forget that coin."

"I beg your pardon, My Lord! It will always prick my conscience if I give up the idea of fetching that coin on account of the allurement of one thousand gold coins given by you."

Now this was something more than too much. The king's ego was hurt.

Innocent Ramdin was determined to go to the forest to fetch his money, so that he could take his wife to the village fair, and now, the king was equally determined not to allow him to go to the forest to fetch that coin, no matter how heavily he may have to compensate in return.

Thinking this he said, "Look Ramdin! I have decided that I shall not allow you to go to fetch that coin, no matter how heavily I may have to pay to change your decision. I am ready to give anything you demand against that silver coin."

"Too much of wealth spoils a person, O Lord! I am a very poor boy. Getting enough to manage our bread and butter is more than sufficient for me. Even your boundless wealth cannot give me the happiness that I shall get from spending that particular silver coin on my wife.

"I am very happy to know your views, Ramdin. I understand you are not greedy. In fact a kingdom which has young boys like you in it, is bound to flourish. I happily offer you half of my kingdom, but with a precondition that you wouldn't go to fetch that silver coin."

The king was determined.

Ramdin understood the king's resolve. He was in a dilemma now. If still he insisted on going to fetch the silver coin, he, instead of getting reward, could get punishment also.

So, it would be better to cling to such a ruse that it may not deprive him of his silver coin and that he may not be subjected to punishment also.

So, he said, "My Lord! I am bound to obey your orders under all circumstances. But I would like to be awarded only that portion of your kingdom that I may select for myself."

"Bravo! Now you are talking wise. Subject's must always obey their king. Now tell me, which portion of my kingdom would you like to be awarded in your favour? I promise to award that very portion."

After giving a careful thinking, Ramdin said—

"I would like to be awarded the northern portion of your kingdom in my favour."

"Oh, Ramdin! You are indeed very wise. Using your wit, you have satisfied me by obeying me, and you managed to get that one-rupee silver coin also, because my old palace is in the northern side of my kingdom where you have hidden your coin. You are not only wise, you are also a boy of firm determination. Young boys like you always rise. It's a matter of pride for me that there are young boys like you in my kingdom."

"I must thank that auspicious coin also due to which you willingly awarded half of your kingdom in my favour, My Lord! Now you please tell me yourself if it would really be wise to make a compromise at the cost of that silver coin."

The King surrendered before the wisdom and power of determination of Ramdin.

On that very day the king awarded the northern portion of his kingdom in favour of Ramdin and declared him the king of that portion.

As soon as he was declared king, Ramdin set out to the old palace. He slid the loose bricks, took out his coin, kissed it and touching it to his forehead he said, "You are extremely great! It is because of you that lady luck has smiled on me. If I had not got you, neither I would have got a beautiful and affable wife like Paro, nor would I have got this kingdom.

6

INSTINCTS NEVER CHANGE

Iᴛ was a very long time ago, when there was a man—Dhanku, who used to commit thievery and manage his bread and butter, thus. He had been arrested many times for this crime. And every time he was arrested, he was awarded punishment by court of law. And every time he came out of the prison, he involved himself in thieving again. Even talking to him was considered below dignity by people. Dhanku was also pained to realise that the kind of act he was involved in, kept him isolated in the society. One day he began thinking that he should discontinue the practice of stealing things and do something that may earn his bread and butter and also that he was not looked down by others in the society. Fed up of his life which had made him the target of hatred by others, he set out in search of some job.

But wherever he went looking for a job, he was shooed away; because there was none in the town who was not aware of his base deeds and profession. Dhanku went to a Seth and said with folded hands, "Seth Ji! I am Dhanku."

"Oh, Dhanku—the thief!"

"Yes, Seth Ji!"

"Go away from here! What have you come here for? You swindler!"

"At least listen to me, Seth Ji!" implored Dhanku. "I have now discontinued the practice of committing thefts. I am fed up of this kind of life. I am a changed man now; I want to lead an ideal life. Please employ me in your shop and trust me, I shall perform all my duties honestly and sincerely. And I shall happily accept whatever you give for the service rendered by me."

"Go away from here. Do you think I am a fool that I shall employ a thief like you. A thief is always dominated by his instincts. No, no, go and see some other shop; there is no place for you in my shop."

Being reprimanded thus, everywhere Dhanku went in search of job, he became very sad. He had taken a solemn pledge that he wouldn't commit thefts anymore; and on the other side he was also not able to get a proper job. Starving and thirsty, he came wandering to a hermitage, where there were many saints busy in their prayers and worship.

Devotees were coming, making their offerings at the feet of the gods and then offering good foods and costly garments to saints.

Seeing all this Dhanku began thinking—'I have wasted all my life for nothing—these saints are much better than me; they eat their fill and live happily in the shelter of God. They are not concerned with anyone; they are not worried about their future; they radiate inner contentment.'

Dhanku thought—'Why not pass the rest of my life as a saint. Neither I would have to worry about meals and clothes nor would I have to fear award of punishment by the royal court; and above all I would be leading a respectable life.' He talked to the hermits, and with their permission, he began living in the hermitage. Day and night he would be at the service of the saints and pass his time in prayers and worship. He had also donned himself in the garments of saints. And now he had become Dhanku Maharaj from Dhanku.

Dhanku Maharaj began living a very comfortable life. Saints

generally are rovers by nature and they wander like vagabonds. One day, the saints decided to go on a pilgrimage and left the hermitage in Dhanku Maharaj's care. Dhanku himself was not interested in wandering like vagabonds. Sitting and eating comfortably was something of his choice.

Meanwhile, in the absence of the saints, thieves and robbers held sway in the village. The thieves and robbers were in such high spirits that they would endeavour to commit thefts and robberis even during day times also. The villagers became extremely worried. Even the chief of the village and the landlord could not feel free from the fear of thievery and robbery.

The landlord was comparatively more worried as apart from thoushds of currency notes, he had gold and silver also in his safe. The main cause of worry was gold and silver in his possession.

After giving a serious thinking, the landlord came to the conclusion that even if the whole of the village is pilfered and robbed, the hermitage will remain safe. The saints have no possessions. Why would a thief go to a hermitage, and what will he get there? As soon as this idea came across his mind, he decided to put all his money, gold and silver in the hermitage, thinking that his treasure would remain absolutely safe in the custody of the care-taker of the hermitage. But then suddenly another thought crept in his mind—'Suppose the saint himself winds up my treasure and slips out of village.'

'No, no, doubting the integrity of saints in this manner is a sin. They are detached people; they have nothing to do with wealth. Their greatest wealth is the name of Lord Rama. They are the true representatives of God."

The landlord was absolutely unaware of the fact that Dhanku Maharaj—the saint—was in fact a thief before joining the company of hermits.

After considering every aspect carefully, the landlord stuffed the gold and silver in a pitcher and brought it to the hermitage of Dhanku Maharaj. He kept the pitcher full of gold and silver in a corner and touched his feet with great reverence.

"May God bless you! Be happy!" Dhanku Maharaj blessed him. "May you live long! May you remain secured."

"How to remain secured, Maharaj?"

"Why, my son? What's the problem?" Dhanku was aware that he was the landlord of the village and if he could be pleased somehow, he would donate a lot of money to the hermitage. So, in order to impress him, Dhanku said, "Tell me your problem and with the blessings of goddess Durga, I shall render you free from all worries."

"That's the reason why I have come in your shelter, Maharaj," said the landlord. "You must be aware that the cases of theft and robbery in the village are on the rise. Ever since this kind of happenings has started taking place, I have been having sleepless nights. Every minute I am worried about the safety of my treasure," the landlord signalled towards the pitcher. "This is my hard-earned wealth and I am worried about its safety. I have never hurt the feelings of any farmer or any labour. Now just imagine, who will call me a landlord, if thieves steal this treasure."

"What you say is correct, my son. Money has its own importance these days." Dhanuk's eyes gleamed seeing the pitcher full of gold and silver. "Anyway, you tell me the reason why you have brought gold and silver in this pitcher to me?"

"Maharaj! I wish you keep this treasure in the hermitage in your custody. No one can steal it from here."

'My dear Dhanku! Lady luck has smiled on you. See this is the glory of your majestic appearance in the disguise of saints. Money itself is coming to you.' Dhanku said to himself. Seeing such huge treasure before his eyes, his instincts once again became active. 'Your days have changed Dhanku. If you manage to escape with this treasure and settle down in some other country, you can lead a comfortable life like rich people.' Dhanku's mouth began watering. But since he was sitting in a saint's disguise, adopting the countenance of saints, he said, "What do you say, my son? How are we concerned with money and gold? Money guides towards sinful acts."

"I agree with you, Maharaj. Spiritual life and worldly life are two altogether different aspects. But, sir! coming to the rescue of devotees is your duty when they are in trouble. Right now I am in trouble because of this treasure and that's the reason why I have come in you shelter. So long as there is no other suitable arrangement for the safety of this treasure, this will remain in your custody as a deposit. This is my humble request."

"Do you really have so much faith in me?"

"Not having faith is simply out of question. And so far as you are concerned, you are the direct incarnation of God. Money and gold can allure a person who is leading worldly life, but a person like you who is leading spiritual life, a person who has dedicated his life to God, can in no way fall victim to worldly allurements."

"You are very innocent, my son," said Dhanku. "Anyway if you have so much faith in me, you do one thing—I won't touch it—take it to the

Peepal tree, dig a pit underneath and bury it there. God will take care of your treasure."

"All right, Maharaj!" said the landlord happily. I shall always remember the favour extended by you to me."

"That's all right, my son. But if you wish to live without any tension in your life you shall have to learn to detach yourself. Try to learn to be content with what you have. A contented person is always happy. And a person who wastes his time in running after materialistic pattern of life, is always unhappy.

"You are great, Maharaj! You are simply too great!"

"That's why I advise you to earn the wealth of contentment."

"I shall always remember your teachings, sir."

"Now go and bury your treasure there. And you may come and take it away any time you like."

"As you wish, Maharaj."

The landlord went to the Peepal tree and began digging a pit underneath with a shovel lying there.

The sanctimonious hypocrite—Dhanku—was seeing all that, and in his heart of hearts he wanted to take away the treasure as soon as possible.

It is then that his soul snubbed him—'Dhanku! what kind of thoughts are you allowing to dominate your mind? Have you forgotten that you have dedicated your life to the service of God. It's a sin for you even to think of such things after having decided to lead a spiritual life.'

'Oh, I took to this ruse only to save myself from going to prison everyday. I disguised myself as a saint because I was hated by everyone as a thief, and no one respected me.'

'But now people have great reverence for you. You are comfortable in every respect. Then what is it that makes you unsteady now?'

'Life has no meaning without money. Wealth and respect are two sides of a coin. Why should I let go such golden chance?'

'But if you sneak off with the treasure of the landlord, it isn't that only you will earn a bad name, rather you will bring bad name to the saints'

community on the whole.'

'How am I concerned with all this? At least I shall lead a comfortable life. I shall shift to some other town and enjoy the luxuries of life.'

Dhanku's soul gave all the logics of prudence, but Dhanku had his own logics and excuses. Now he was only waiting for the right opportunity to sneak off with the treasure of the landlord.

After some time the landlord came back and said, "Maharaj! I have buried the treasure as directed by you."

"All right, my son! Now forget all your worries and go home."

The landlord returned home happily. Now he was confident about the safety of his treasure. He had full faith in the saint.

Many days passed thus. The landlord used to pass major period of the day in the hermitage, ever since he had buried his treasure there. Everytime he came to the hermitage, he brought dainty dishes for Dhanku Maharaj and discussed spiritual matters with him.

The landlord's visit to the hermitage everyday had deprived Dhanku Maharaj of the opportunity to sneak off with his treasure. But he had planned many thing's in his imagination—marriage, a magnificent building, and childern, and so many other things.

Once the landlord fell ill. This was the best opportunity for Dhanku to sneak off with the treasure. On the same night he dug up the pitcher, full of gold and silver, from out of the ground. He bundled it with his own belongings and set out to the landlord's house to tell him to take care of his treasure and that he was leaving the place.

'Dhanku!' rose a voice from his soul. 'Suppose the landlord comes to take back his treasure immediately after you inform him of your plan of departure...? What will happen?'

'Nothing will happen. I shall plainly tell him that he should look for his treasure in the place where he had hidden it. For us saints it was as good as clay. Some thief might have stolen it.'

'Give a second thought, Dhanku! What you are doing is highly improper. You have achieved this reverence with great difficulty. Your greed for treasure may return you to the same kind of old life.'

Now, you have to take at least some risk in order to have possession of such a valuable treasure.'

Dhanku's visit to his house surprised the landlord greatly.

'Maharaj! You! You could have summoned me if you needed something.'

"Look, my son! I am leaving the hermitage and going away. My only wish is that you go and take possession of your treasure."

"But Maharaj! What made you decide to leave this place all of a sudden? And above all, who will look after the hermitage after you go away?"

"My son! It is God who takes care of everything. And so far as I am concerned, saints are like water and air who can never be stationary."

"Please have your seat, Maharaj. Let me arrange some light food for you."

"No, I cannot wait another minute. The gorges of the Himalayas are calling me."

The landlord became very sad to learn that one whom he had entrusted the safety of his treasure was going away. Once again he was worried. With great difficulty he managed to become normal and came out to see the saint off.

"Maharaj!" said the landlord at the gate of his mansion, "Once again I make a request to you with folded hands to change your decision. Please don't leave this village and the hermitage. Please don't deprive this village of your grand presence."

"Come what may, my child! But I cannot change my decision. Now hurry up! go to the hermitage and take possession of your treasure."

"As you wish, Maharaj!" said the landlord with folded hands.

Dhanku was thinking that he had committed minor thefts many times, but this was for the first time that he had had the opportunity to thieve a sizeable chunk of wealth. Suddenly Dhanku thought—'it's quite likely that I shift to some other town and settle down there, and the landlord also comes to the same town for some work and seeing me there, he may report the matter and get me arrested. So I must do something to build deep trust in him for me. Thinking this Dhanku stuck a straw in his hair and returned to the mansion.

The landlord looked at him with surprise.

"What happened, Maharaj! Is it that I made some mistake that you had to come back?"

"No, no, my child! You haven't made any mistake," said Dhanku. "In fact a straw of your mansion got stuck in my hair and I was going away with it. You already know, my child! That I don't accept even a straw from anyone. All that I want is contentment. And that's the reason why I came back to return your straw." Saying this Dhanku Maharaj took out the straw from his hair and handing it over to the landlord, he departed.

"You are great, Maharaj! Indeed you are great! It's hard to believe that still there are saints on this earth who don't accept even a straw from anyone."

Once again the landlord seemed to be greatly impressed by Dhanku Maharaj.

A friend of the landlord also happened to be sitting there who had come to know of his well-being. He was a shrewd person. Dhanku Maharaj's hypocrisy caused some doubt in his mind.

So, he asked his friend, "What is all thism my friend?"

"Raghuraj! The saint you saw just now, is a revealed soul. You are already aware how thieves and robbers had held saway in this village. And there came a point of time when I had begun feeling very unsafe. So, one day I took all my gold and silver in a pitcher and buried it in his hermitage under a Peepal tree. My treasure was in his custody till now. He is very simple and gentle. He had come all the way to tell me that I should go and take possession of my treasure because he is going on a pilgrimage."

"And what was the 'straw' business? What a great farce?"

"Oh, Raghu! you call it a farce! This is rather a very small proof of his honesty. Didn't you see that not even a straw of someone's house is acceptable to him."

Raghuraj suddenly burst into laughter.

"Why are you laughing? Is it something to be laughed at?" he became irritable to see his friend laughing suddenly.

"You are very simple, my friend!"

"What makes you say that?"

"Friend! This saint seems to be a sanctimonious hypocrite to me. He is a big cheat."

"For God's sake, don't talk like this. Make sure of your statement before you say something about someone."

"I have considered every aspect before saying this, my friend. You are being cheated. This saint, who is trying to prove his honesty in so many ways, is in fact a cheat. Real saints don't have to prove their honesty everywhere."

"For you everyone is a cheat," said the landlord with confidence. "Take your words back, Raghuraj, or else you shall have to bear the consequences. Maharaj is a great saint; one should not say such things about revealed souls."

"I am ready to bear any consequences, but I am determined to bring the truth before your eyes. Tell me, where is your treasure?"

"In the hermitage, under a Peepal tree."

"But it won't be there."

"But why?"

"Because this saint has some motives. And that's the reason why he was creating all this farce. Had he been truthful, he would have had your treasure dug up from out of the ground, handed it over to you and then would have talked about his departure. Come with me at once if you wish to save your treasure."

"But..."

"No ifs and buts!" said Raghuraj pulling the hand of the landlord towards the door. "You will have to repent if you delayed anymore.

"But..."

The landlord tried to say something, but Raghuraj didn't listen to him.

Within a short time they were in the hermitage. None was to be

seen there.

"O God! Where is Dhanku Maharaj?"

"Not Dhanku Maharaj. Call him a cheat. He has taken away your hard-earned money."

"Oh, God! I hope not! I shall be ruined."

"First you tell me the exact place where you had buried the pitcher."

"Under this Peepal tree."

"All right! Dig it up immediately. I am confident your treasure is not there; but still...do it for your satisfaction."

Hearing this the landlord was bathed in cold sweat. Now the absence of the saint created a doubt in his mind also. "I wish what my friend says is not true." Saying this he took a shovel lying in the corner and began digging the spot quickly. The earth, where he had buried his treasure was very soft. It seemed someone had dug up the pit and again stuffed it with earth after taking out the pitcher.

Within no time he had dug the pit quite deep, but his pitcher was not to be seen anywhere. Just then a string of beeds got stuck to the blade of the shovel.

The landlord picked it up and said, "How did it come here? This string of beeds belongs to Dhanku Maharaj. Raghuraj! This is very surprising; because it was I who dug the pit and buried the treasure here."

"I think, that hypocrite must have dropped it here by mistake while taking out the pitcher and because of his greed for the treasure, he might not have noticed it."

"Oh, my God!" The landlord was shocked. "I am ruined. My life-time hard-earned money has been stolen away, my friend."

"Being nervous in this manner is not going to serve your purose. We must move fast and get him. I am sure he has not gone too far. Come on! Quick!"

The landlord was sweating and trembling nervously. He had been thoroughly cheated. He had never seen a devil in the guise of a saint.

"Don't let your heart sink. You are not going to get anything out of losing your courage. Just be normal and come with me."

Then both moved towards the forest as fast as their legs could take. Raghuraj was confident that the thief would try to make his escape through the forest only.

They were running and panting; they were sweating like bullocks, but it was the primacy of acquiring the treasure from the clutches of the thief that exhorted them to run still faster. After they had covered quite a distance, running and panting, they saw a silhouette moving on a narrow track at a distance.

"Look!" shouted Raghuraj shrilly. "Your Dhanku Maharaj—the sanctimonious hypocrite is running."

Dhanku heard the voice and turned back to see. He looked timidly at them his heart in his mouth. It was difficult for him to run fast with his own belongings and the pitcherful of gold and silver on his back. His plan had failed. He thought—'Why not throw away the pitcher and manage to escape?' Then he thought—'No, no, they are still at quite a distance. They won't be able to catch me.'—Thinking this he began running faster.

But how long could he run! At last the landlord and Raghuraj caught hold of him and took him in their grips.

"You, hypocrite! you, thief! A devil in the guise of saint! You were running away with my life-time hard-earned money. Wait, we will teach you the lesson of life.

Raghuraj caught him by his hair with one hand and began beating him with the other. Seeing no alternative, Dhanku also threw aside the pitcher and began fighting with Raghuraj in self-defence.

But this fight was not proportionately balanced; the landlord and Raghuraj were two in number, whereas Dhanku was alone. Finally, he was overpowered by them and beaten almost to death.

"You, Sinner! I had great reverence for you. I almost went to the extent of worshipping you. But this is how you have responded to my reverence for you. You, wicked person! You have brought bad name to the community of saints also."

"Please forgive me, sir! it is greed that dominated my thoughts and made me commit this sin. I promise in the name of God that there won't be recurrence of this kind in future. Please forgive me," Dhanku implored.

"You will be set right only after you are put behind bars," said Raghuraj. "Friend! Take him and hand him over to police."

Dhanku was greatly terrified to hear the name of prison. Till now he had been involved in small pilferage and had been put behind bars so many times; but this time he was sure that he would rot in prison throughout his life, if handed over to police by the landlord. Thinking this he decided to make an escape.

Dhanku gave a sudden jerk and freed himself from the clutches of the landlord and Raghuraj; and before they could understand anything, Dhanku had already entered the thorny bushes of the dense forest.

The landlord and his friend did not even try to chase him. The landlord was happy to get his treasure back and Raghuraj was happy that, with his extraordinary perception, he could manage to save the treasure of his friend from being stolen.

"Raghuraj!" spoke the landlord after a long silence—"I have a request, my friend."

"What is it?"

"All the saints are not hypocrites! If you make a mention of this happening to people, they will lose their faith in saints."

"What you say is correct, my friend. The whole of the saints' community should not earn a bad name because of this sanctimonious hypocrite."

And both the friends set out to their village.

❑ ❑

7

REWARD OF HOSPITALITY

IN Madhopur village, there lived a labourer whose name was Bhlolaram. He was very poor but very simple. 'Honesty and hard work' was the motto of his life. He would go out in search of job everyday, work hard, and put all his earning in the hands of his wife every evening. The amount he earned everyday was so meagre that he could hardly manage to earn a square meal for his family and for himself; and thinking of making charities was something beyond dreams for him. People would generally call him miserly and selfish; but Bholaram would never take ill of such remarks.

One morning, as soon as he left his house in search of job, he saw the chief of village sitting with villagers in the assembly hall, engrossed in serious discussion over something. Some villagers were busy cleaning the big ground by the side of the assembly hall.

Bhola was greatly surprised to see all this. He began thinking—'There definitely is something special; that's why the whole of the village has assembled here. I should go and enquire from the chief of village.

Thinking this, he advanced towards the chief.

"Good morning, Chief!"

"Come, Bhola! Come! Good morning!" said the chief and continued his discussion—"Yes, Chamanlal! will you take the responsibility of twenty people?"

"Yes, Chief!"

"Please fifty one people against my name in your book," said another one.

"O God! what is all this? What responsibilities are being fixed?" Bhola began thinking.

The Chief was busy in his work. "Brother, Sitaram! Arranging Pandal is your responsibility. I hope you remember."

"Yes, chief!"

"And brother, Ramprasad! What is it that you want?"

"Chief! I shall be able to take care of ten-twelve saints only."

"All right! I am putting ten saints against your name in my book."

Bhola was becoming increasingly curious. He asked, "Chief! What is this all about? What are you writing in your book?"

"O Bhola! You don't know? I had made an announcement in the village last night."

"What announcement, chief!" Bhola was in a tense situation. He began thinking—'There was an announcement last night, and I have no knowledge of it?"

"Look, brother! A highly realised soul, a great saint is coming to our village with his one thousand disciples. On their way to their destination on pilgrimage, they will be making a one-day halt in our village. We are making arrangements for extending proper hospitality to him and his disciples. It will be our moral responsibility to make suitable arrangements for their fooding and lodging. There is no binding on anyone. Everyone is free to decide the number of saints he can take care of. It's all a matter of dedication and capability."

"It's the good luck of us all that a highly realised saint is coming to our village."

"Now you tell me the number of saints, you can take care of," said the chief coming to the main issue. "Ramlal has agreed to attend on thirty one saints; Chaman Lal has offered to attend on twenty saints, and Sitaram will be responsible for complete arrangement of Pandal. You tell me about yourself."

Bhola became sad to hear this.

He said with folded hands, "Chief! I too like to participate in the activities of charity; but you already know how poor I am. Even my landed property is mortgaged with the money-lender for the last so many years. I can hardly manage to arrange meals for my children even."

The chief became a little unhappy to hear this. He said, "Bhola! Do you want to know why you are so poor? Have you ever thought that despite working hard day and night, you are neither able to save money, nor you can take care of your family properly?"

"I know, sir! It's all my ill-fate that I sweat my blood day and night and still I am hand-to-mouth," said Bhola in a choked voice.

"Bhola! This is not ill-fate. The bitter truth of life is that a selfish man never prospers. And I have no hesitation in calling you a selfish man."

"I am selfish?" Bhola was shocked to hear the remarks of the chief. "What are you saying, sir? A selfish man is a person who harms others for his own selfish ends; and believe me, sir, I have done no harm to anyone in my life."

"Bhola! It's not that one who does harm to others to serve his selfish ends, is selfish; one who thinks about oneself only, is also selfish. And for you, your family is the only concern; you never think of others; you don't care for the well-being of others."

Bhola was getting shocks after shocks. There were others also standing near him; everyone giving a strange look.

Bhola was greatly insulted. He said, "Sir, What you say is correct. It is true that I have never cared to think about others except my family. And perhaps that's the reason why prosperity has never fallen in my share. Sir, I promise to rectify my mistake from today. I won't be able to do much, but still, please note down in your book against my name, the expenses to be borne by me for one saint. Even if I have to go hungry, I shall extend hospitality to one saint, at least."

Meanwhile, the money-lender arrived there, and Bhola was sidetracked. He was almost pushed aside. The chief stood in a gesture of respect for the money-lender.

"Come, Seth Ji! come."

"Chief! Why have you given the responsibility of the saints to so many people of the village? At least, so long as I am in the village, No one needs to bother. I alone am capable of taking care of all the saints."

"I agree, Seth Ji, but it won't be just; the village assembly has decided last night that every villager should participate in this activity of religious merit, so that none is deprived of the reward of performing the virtuous deed."

"Dear chief! If this is what the village assembly has decided, I am ready to abide by the verdict; but, now please do me a favour—kindly allow me to extend my hospitality to the remaining saints, the responsibility of whom has not been allotted to anyone yet."

"All right! Seth Ji!" The chief accepted the proposal of the money-lender.

Bhola was left isolated. He was feeling very insulted.

"It is only the moneyed people who hold respectable position in the society," Bhola began thinking. "I wish, I too had been rich. Anyway, sooner or later God does respond. I shall go and tell my wife to make suitable arrangements, so that I am not found lacking in extending hospitality to my guest. And this I shall do, no matter how hard I have to work for this purpose.

Thinking this Bholaram began moving toward his house.

Bholaram's wife was busy stitching some old garment in her courtyard. She was surprised to see Bhola return so soon. She said, "How is it that you have come back so early? Either you didn't go in search of job or perhaps you didn't get any job today."

"No, no, dear! The truth is that I have not yet been able to go out in search of job."

His wife Laxmi looked at him in surprise and said, "Look, there is nothing for us to eat in the house today. If you don't go out to earn we shall have to starve today."

"Have faith in God; everything will be all right. But first you tell me if there had been any announcement last night."

"Yes, there had been an announcement and it was announced that some one thousand saints are coming to our village, and it was expected of everyone in the village to come forward and offer to perform the solemn duty of extending hospitality to our honourable guests. And the chief had also desired that every male member of the village should collect in the assembly hall in the morning."

"But you didn't tell me anything."

"What was the use of telling you? What you earn is not sufficient even for us; taking extra burden or making charities is beyond reach for us."

"Darling, we are in this kind of situation, because we think of ourselves only; we don't think about others. God Himself creates suitable means for those who have the intentions of making charities. Look, some one thousand saints are coming to our village with Swamy Ji. Everyone in the village has offered to extend hospitality to certain number of saints according to his capability. I too have offered to take care of one saint for his fooding and lodging for one day. I shall work as hard as possible today, but I shall, in any case, make suitable arrangements for his meals. We shall not allow our guest to go without meals, even if we have to starve."

"All right! If this is what you wish, I shall not allow you to go alone today, you will be accompanied by me. We shall leave no stone unturned in taking care of our guest."

"You are great! This is what I had expected of you." Bhola was extremely pleased to hear her reply. He said, "Don't worry! Everything will be all right. God will help us execute our responsibility."

Now Bhola was feeling quite relieved. He was full of new kind of energy. His face was transfixed in ecstacy; he was filled with great enthusiasm, and a great deal of self-confidence.

Within a short time, both, husband and wife, set out in search of job. Both were praying—"God! please help us get some good job in order to enable us to render the best possible hospitality to our coming guest. God! please help us save our prestige before the villagers."

A person, whether poor or rich, is always very conscious of self-prestige. One doesn't like to be looked down by others.

Lost in their thoughts, they were wandering in search of job, when they heard someone calling from inside the house—"O Bhola! Please wait for a minute."

Bhola and his wife stopped.

Within moments, appeared the money-lender at the gate of his house. He said, "Where are you going, Bhola?"

"I am going in search of job, sir."

"It's long since you haven't paid your debts. Now the position is that the land you have mortgaged, doesn't yield enough crops to meet the amount of interest even."

"Liar, blood sucker! This swine has taken away my oxen along with my landed property and still I owe him money," thought Bhola to himself, but said, "Seth Ji, please don't worry about the debt. God willing, I shall repay each and every pice of the debt. Is this the reason why you had stopped me?"

"No, no! Not at all!" simpered the money-lender and said, "I stopped you because some guests are coming to my house tomorrow, and I have no fuel in my house. If you cut some firewood for me, I shall make payment to your demand."

"Shall we have to bring the firewood from Jungle?"

"No, no! I have got logs; you only have to cut them into small pieces, so that it can be used as fuel. Will you do it for me?"

"I shall definitely do it, Seth Ji. Please don't worry about it."

"But all the logs should be cut by the evening today."

"I shall do it, Seth Ji. I shall definitely do it."

Bhola was very happy that he didn't have to go too far in search of job; he got the job in the village itself. 'Now I don't have to wander around; also the money-lender is not miserly. He will pay handsomely. Thought Bhola. 'At least now, I shall be able to take good care of the saint with the money that I shall earn today.'

The money-lender took Bhola in his backyard and showed him the big pile of logs lying there.

"Seth Ji! Do I have to cut all these?"

"Yes, Bhola!"

Bhola began thinking—'It's such a big pile, and there is hardly any possibility of my being able to finish the job by evening.'

But he was helpless.

He had to cut the logs by evening, because he had to make appropriate arrangements for the guest, and there was not even a single grain of rice available in his house.

Anyway...he remembered the Almighty and picked up his axe.

He sent his wife back, because his wife could not share the job he had undertaken to do.

Once Bhola began chopping the logs, he continued doing it till evening.

By evening there was a big pile of firewood lying before him, but still there were many log's left to be chopped.

Bhola was completely exhausted and sweating like a bullock.

His body began aching with tremendous pain. It seemed he had lost all his vital energy. He almost felt like throwing aside the axe and lying down on the pile of firewood. But despite wanting to lie down and take rest, he couldn't do so, as he was aware of the fact that the money-

lender won't make payment until he had chopped all the logs.

His hands were bleeding profusely, but he did not pay any attention to it. There was only one thing on his mind that the saint, who was going to be his guest next day, had to be entertained with complete dedication; and it was this feeling of dedication that was filling him with great enthusiasm.

Bhola was so busy chopping the logs that he did not even notice when it became dark. The money-lender was standing in a corner watching Bhola. He was full of praise for him.

At last Bhola had chopped all the logs. he looked at the money-lender, threw aside his axe and lay on the pile of firewood almost dead. He was so terribly tired and his body had become so lifeless that he could hardly stand on his feet

"Oh, God! Please give me energy." These were the words he uttered feebly and fell unconscious.

His pitiable condition created a wave of sympathy in the heart of the money-lender. He sprinkled cold water on the face of Bhola and brought him back to conscionsness.

"Bhola! You are indeed very hard working. You have done alone something that even five men wouldn't have been able to do in a day. I am extremely happy with you. The labour charge that I shall pay will equal the amount of the labour change of five men; so that you could take care of your guest suitably tomorrow.

Saying this the money-lender went inside.

There were two servants with him when he returned after some time. One had a basket full of rice in his hands, and the other one had a basket in his hands which was full of fruits and vegetables.

"Bhola! This is all yours."

Bhola was looking at the baskets wide-eyed. He had never expected to get so much for his work.

"This is all the result of your hard work. In fact my wife had bet me that no human being was capable of chopping such a big pile of logs in a day. And I was of the view that it was the need that could make a person do even the impossible. A person in dire need of money would chop even double the quantity of logs in a day. Meanwhile I happened to see you and decided to get the job done by you. I knew you were in need of money for tomorrow; and, Bhola! it is because of you that I have won the bet. I am givng you all this happily. Since you have saved my prestige, I feel it is also my duty to save your prestige. Please accept it."

"It is true, Seth Ji! I had to make arrangements for the guest coming tomorrow; and I had left my house thinking that I shall work very hard to earn so much that could be sufficient for extending hospitality to my guest; but what you have given is more than what I deserve."

"No, no! Not at all Bhola! You fully deserve it."

Bhola couldn't say much. Though he was extremely tired, he somehow managed to take both the baskets in his hands and began walking feebly towards his house. He was mumbling in low tone—'God! You are great. You are just great.'

Bhola's wife was greatly surprised when she saw Bhola with baskets of rice, fruits and vegetables.

"What is this, dear? You seem to have bought the whole market."

"No, dear! I haven't bought all this."

"Then?"

"This is what the money-lender has given me for the hard work done by me today, Luxmi! Now I feel that God is very kind to us. I think this is the miracle of the saint who is going to come to our house tomorrow as our guest. God gives prosperity to those who develop a feeling for others. It is the dedication towards the cause of others that makes him happy."

"What you say is correct, dear. I fully agree with you. Just think—we have not made an iota of charity so far, and God has been so kind to give us so much for one day's work; and how happy and prosperous we shall become, once we start making charities. Now I have decided once for all that I shall not let any saint or needy go empty-handed from my house. Anyway...please get fresh and have your meals; you must be terribly tired."

"I am indeed very tired, Luxmi," said Bhola with a smile. "But I don't know why my tiredness is not being able to dominate my enthusiasm. My only worry is to entertain my guest tomorrow. May God help me!"

"It so will happen, my dear! Leave everything to Him. He will manage everything suitably."

"You are right, Luxmi!"

Both, husband and wife, had their meals and went to sleep; but the worry for extending hospitality to their guest kept them awake and they kept changing sides throughout the night.

As soon as they got up in the morning, they saw a man standing at the gate of their house.

"I have heard you have arranged to give a feast today."

"Feast?" Bhola was surprised. "What feast?"

"Are you not going to offer meals to some saint today?"

"Oh, yes! That's true."

"Then, in that case, please engage me as a servant for today."

"Servant? Are you kidding? I myself am very poor. How can I engage a servant?"

"I shall not charge you for my labour, if you are poor; but please engage me."

"Look, brother! Why don't you try some other house? It is against my temperament to get anything done by someone free of charge. People would laugh at me and say—'This guy doesn't have enough for himself and he has engaged a servant."

"Brother! I have come from a village nearby. I have heard that some saints are coming to this village. I wish to offer may humble service to those saints. And you cannot deprive me of my right of rendering my service to them."

Saying this he entered the house without caring to take their permission.

Both, husband and wife, were simply amazed. They could not understand all this. And turning out this uninvited guest sternly, was also they could never afford to do. The stranger became busy in the kitchen without any delay.

"Leave it!" said Bhola to Luxmi. "We should take all this as the will of God; and there is no alternative also. Come on! Let's go inside."

When Luxmi entered the kitchen the stranger began helping her. And Bhola went to take bath.

After some time when he returned after bath, his wife said, "The food is ready; please tell the saint, our respectable guest, to come and have his meals."

"Right away, my dear!"

When Bhola came out of the house, he saw uncharacterstic delight and joviality all over the village. Saints covered with sheets inscribed with Lord Rama's name, were moving all around. Those who had offered to entertain saints, were taking them to their homes with reverence.

Some saints, who were on fast, were imparting discourses in different places. Children, elders and women were listening to their

discourses with devotion. A wave of devotion rose in the heart of Bhola also.

He went to the chief in a hurry and said, "Sir, everything is ready now, and I shall feel highly obliged to attend upon my reverend guest."

"Oh, Bhola!" as if the chief remembered something, seeing Bhola before him. "I am sorry I had forgotten to write down your name in the list of those who had offered to entertain our guests. I hope you remember Seth Badriprasad, who arrived and offered to entertain the remaining guests, just when I was going to enter your name in the list."

Bhola was greatly disappointed to hear this. He felt as if someone had thrown cold water on his plans and enthusiasm. He flew into a fury and said, "Now you yourself tell me, chief, the course of action that I should adopt. What should I do? Listen! so long as a saint does not come to my house and accept my hospitality, neither I nor my wife will eat or drink anything."

"Brother Bhola!" I am indeed very sorry for my mistake and sincerely apologize. You do one thing—make an offering to God and fancy that you have entertained a guest."

"No, no! This is impossible. You have thrown cold water on all my hopes." Tears welled up in Bhola's eyes. He said, "I know, You have not cared to put my name in your list because I am poor."

"Look, brother! Being rich or poor is no consideration in this case. But still, I admit that I have committed a mistake, and I am indeed very sorry for it. All right! Do one thing—go and make a request to some saint, and if he agrees, take him home and entertain him."

Bhola didn't say anything and returned with tears in his eyes. Nothing could please him at this time; he was so disgusted.

Suddenly he heard a sweet voice of a saint—

"One should never lose hopes. Whatever happens is divine wish."

Bhola looked up and saw a saint sitting on a high mound, preaching the villagers. There was a huge crowd around him.

Bhola thought—'Why not take him home and offer him meals. I am sure he will not disappoint me. Thinking this Bhola went to the saint and fell in his feet. He spoke with tears in his eyes in a choked voice— 'Maharaj! Please fulfil my wish; please be kind to accept my offer.'

"What's your problem, my child?"

"I am in great distress, Maharaj."

"The whole world is in distress, my child."

"But my grief is of a different kind, Maharaj." Bhola said, "In fact I am greatly disappointed."

And thus Bhola explained to him everything.—He said, "Now my only submission is that I request you to be kind to me and accept my invitation. Please come to my house and accept whatever little I have. It is only then that I shall get peace."

"If that's what you want, I shall be only too pleased to accept your invitation, my child. I understand you have a selfless devotion and

97

dedication; and I appreciate it. I am very happy."

Hearing the saint, the whole of the gathering was stunned.

In fact, the saint who had accepted the invitation of Bhola so easily, had declined the invitation of the money-lender. This came like a shock to everyone.

And soon this news spread like wildfire all around that the saint, who had shown his disinclination to accept the invitation of the money-lender, was going to Bhola's house as his guest.

People thronged to his house out of curiosity.

The money-lender was terribly shocked to hear this. He took it as an insult to him, and set out to Bhola's house. He wanted to know what had made the saint decline his invitation and accept Bhola's offer.

On the other side, when people saw a cook in the kitchen of Bhola, they were surprised all the more.

"That's strange! Some cook is cooking in Bhola's house. Isn't this a miracle? Has Bhola got some buried treasure?"

People standing outside were expressing their own views; and inside the house, Bhola and his wife were serving dainty dishes to the saint with great devotion.

As soon as the saint came out having finished his meals, the money-lender came and stood before him.

"Maharaj! I want to know why you refused to accept my invitation, and agreed to accept the offer made by Bhola."

"Listen! If you really wish to know the reason—There was ego in your invitation; you wanted the people of the village to see that you could entertain five hundred saints. You wanted to show that you are the only one who could afford to spend so much on the fooding and lodging of saints. Whereas Bhola invited me humbly and earnestly. He has true reverence for saints; and it's only because he is simple and honest."

"You are great, Maharaj!" Bhola became emotional. "I really consider myself lucky that you kindly accepted to take food in the house of a poor man like me."

"Bhola! There isn't anything like rich or poor. God Himself comes on the earth to help those who are truthful, sincere, and honest. Your cook too..."

"My cook? Maharaj! I cannot afford to engage someone. This gentleman himself came to my house with a purpose to render his service to saints." Then turning towards the cook, he said, "Go brother, your wish has been fulfilled. Take the blessings of Maharaj, go home and be happy."

"Yes, Bhola! Now I have to go. But before I leave, I bless you to always remain happy." Suddenly that man began flying in the air, and said, "I am Lord Indra! It is only you in the village who has true devotion for saints, and you did everything selflessly. Everyone else in the village extended hospitality to saints with self-interest. This is the reason why God sent me for your help. I once again bless you to be happy and prosperous.

And within no time Lord Indra disappeared. The saint also disappeared while the people were bowing before Lord Indra. Only his footprints were left.

Realising that it were God and Lord Indra themselves who took meals in their house, tears of happiness began sparkling in their eyes.

❏ ❏

8

GREED IS THE WORST OF ALL EVILS

A very long time ago, there lived a Brahmin named Chandradatta in Kashipur village. He was very wise and virtuous. He also had a disciple who served him day and night. He and his disciple managed with what they got everyday after their routine worship. The villagers were neither rich nor did they believe in charities. Everytime they performed some religious rites through Chandradatta, it was only, when they had no alternative. So, sometimes Chandradatta and his disciple would go without meals also.

Not getting a square meal sometimes, kept Chandradatta worried about his future. Sometimes he would think that he might have to see bad days in his old age if he didn't save money for the future; people won't care to ask for a drop of water even in his bad days.

So, one day Pandit Chandradatta called his disciple and said, "Gangaram! It's very difficult to survive in this village; I have decided to leave this village and shift to the neighbouring country Veerpur; because I have heard that the king and the subjects of that country make charities open heartedly. My son! If you wish you may stay in this village."

"Panditji! What shall I do in this village without you. I shall also accompany you."

"All right! In that case we are leaving tomorrow. You start making preparations for departure."

"As you wish, Panditji." And Gangaram became busy in making preparations for journey.

Within few hours Gangaram bundled up necessary clothing and food and said to Chandradatta—"Panditji! You haven't told me the place where we shall stay in the neighbouring country. Do you have acquaintance with some one there?"

"I have no acquaintance there, but the king of that country—Veer Pratap Singh—is a man of great wisdom, and believes in charity. He will definitely help us establish somewhere; and I am sure we shall get some honourable position in his court also."

"But, Panditji! Will the Brahmins of that country allow us settle down in that place so easily?"

"My son! We are not going there for a debate." Panditji explained to him—"Nor is it our purpose to deprive them of their source of bread and butter. We shall only gain his favour on the basis of our knowledge and wisdom. I am confident that I shall be given complete hounour, once he comes to know of my command over Vaidarbha Mantra."

"Panditji! If what you say is true, why don't you yourself take the advantage of this Mantra?"

"My son! Others can be benefitted by this Mantra; but I myself cannot benefit myself with it. This is the peculiarity of this Mantra. The knower of this Mantra will die as soon as he tries to make use of it, in order to serve his own ends."

"Then why don't you stay here and extend the benefits of this Mantra to someone of this village. After all, this is our village."

"I agree with you; but people in this village are very selfish, and it is because of this reason that I am fed up with them. Whereas, king Veer Pratap Singh is not only virtuous, he is also wise and believes in charity. I strongly wish to extend the benefits of this Mantra to him only."

"All right! Panditji! You must have considered every aspect before coming to this decision."

"Taking decisions is in the hands of human beings, but God only knows what will happen tomorrow. It is quite possible that our wishes may not be fulfilled; but, come what may, it is well decided that we are not going to stay here."

It had become clear to Gangaram that their days were going to change. He was aware that Panditji had mastery over a Mantra, with the help of which, he could make diamonds and pearls pour in heaps. And the value of diamonds and pearls is best known to kings only. This will unable him to attain a very high post also in the court of the king.

×   ×   ×

Next day Panditji and his disciple set out on their journey.

The journey was long and tiring and also there was a dense forest in the way. So, they wanted to reach a safe place in the other country before the fall of night. There were very dangerous robbers in the forest, who used to kill the passers-by and take away their belongings. But Chandradatta was carefree, thinking that no one would rob a poor person like him. Of course, the fear of wild animals was there.

By noon they had entered the forest.

"Panditji! this forest is very frightening. It's so dense a forest that not even the sun seems to be reaching here."

"Yes, my child! We have to cross this forest as soon as possible."

"There must be great danger of robbers and thieves here."

"Yes! But what will they get from us? In fact the real danger is of wild animals."

They were walking speedily talking to each other, When they suddenly heard a harsh voice—"Halt!"

They stopped abruptly and began looking around with great fear in their eyes. They wre in a fix and didn't know who had commanded them to halt.

All of a sudden they heard the sound of horse's hooves.

"Robbers!" said Gangaram trembling with fear.

"Yes, but don't fear; we have nothing that they could snatch from us."

"But, Panditji! I have heard that they kill those who don't have anything with them."

"Giving and taking life is in the hands of God; have faith in Him."

Within moments, a band of robbers came before them. The chief of robbers was riding on a white horse. He had an unsheathed sword in his hand, smeared with blood. He was Madhosingh.

"Where are you going, Pandit?"

"Madhosingh! I am going to king Veer Pratap Singh, king of Veerpur."

"But you shall have to pay my tax before you go to see him—one thousand gold coins'"

"What are you saying, Madhosingh? How can this poor Brahmin have so much money? We manage our bread and butter with charities made by our hosts."

"How did you dare enter this forest, if you didn't have money?" Madhosingh shouted angrily.

"Everyone knows that crossing this forest without paying my tax is impossible. Prepare yourself to die, if you don't have money."

"No, no, sir! Please don't kill my mentor; I have none except him," implored Gangaram.

"Look, my dear! if you really wish that I should spare the life of Panditji, you shall have to arrange one thousand gold coins somehow."

"But where shall I bring so big an amount from?" Gangaram was almost on the verge of weeping.

"Madhosingh!" said Pandit Chandradatta, "This is unjust. Poor Brahmins depend on alms. If you really wish to recover your tax from us, make me perform some religious rites for yourself—and don't pay anything in return."

"We don't believe in this kind of dealings, Pandit. Listen, Gangaram! If you want your mentor's life to be spared, go immediately to the king of Veerpur and tell him that your mentor's life is in danger. I am sure he will give you one thousand gold coins to save the precious life of a learned Brahmin."

"But, Madhosingh! King Veer Pratap Singh does not even know me."

"He may not be knowing you, but he is a king who has faith in religion; and I am sure he will not mind giving you so meagre an amount in order to save the life of a Brahmin."

"All right! I am going," said Gangaram, "but please don't say anything to my mentor, so long as I don't come back."

"Yes, we agree; so long as you don't return, we shall keep your mentor tied to this tree. If you bring money; he will be freed, or else, he will have to lose his life."

"All right!" Gangaram agreed to abide by the precondition laid by the chief of robbers, and said to Pandit Chandradatta—"Sir, please don't worry; I shall go and explain everything to king veer Pratap Singh and I shall also tell him that you have command over Vaidarbha Mantra. Once he is freed by the robbers, he will extend great benefits with the help of this Mantra to you. So long, manage to keep yourself safe from these beasts."

"All right! My son! I am confident, king Veer Pratap Singh will definitely save my life and free me from the clutches of these robbers."

"But, Sir! Never tell them anything about Vaidarbha Mantra; because I am sure these robbers won't leave you even after their demand is fulfilled," saying this Gangaram touched his feet.

Panditji blessed him and said, "You too take care of yourself, my son."

"See you, sir!" said Gangaram, and then he spoke to the chief of robbers—"Kindly arrange a horse for me, so that I can arrange money for you early."

"All right! Mangal Singh! Give him a horse."

And then Gangaram set out on his journey. He was worried about Pandit Chandradatta—his mentor. He wanted to save his life at any cost.

Panditji was tied to a tree after Gangaram left.

Pandit Chandradatta, though sent his protege, he was sure that he won't be able to arrange gold-coins; because king Veer Pratap Singh neither knew him nor his protege—Gangaram. So, Why would he give him one thousand gold-coins just for going and explaining to him the difficult situation that I am in. He was confident that the robbers would kill him; but he was happy that at least, he had allowed Gangaram to escape, and thus save his life.

×　　　　　　×　　　　　　×

Time was rolling on and Panditji could see the time of his death nearing him. Panditji began thinking—'Suppose, worse comes to worst, and Gangaram doesn't succeed in arranging the money to pay the ransom, these robbers would kill me—What would happen to my Vaidarbha Mantra? I must not ignore the primacy of the safety of my life. Why not take advantage of this Mantra? This Mantra is effective only once in a year. I shall extend the benefits of this Mantra to the king next year. Right now I must think of the safety of my life.'

"Why did you let Gangaram go, if that was so?" asked Panditji to himself.

"It didn't occur to me then; still it's not too late. If he doesn't return with one thousand gold-coins, I shall make use of this Mantra. But I must wait for Gangaram," Panditji consoled himself.

The sun set in the evening and it started getting dark as the night fell. Panditji, tied to the tree, was eagerly awaiting Gangaram. The robbers settled around the tree. The robbers had liquor and roasted meat for dinner. Panditji detested the very smell of it. Somehow he managed to pass the night.

Tied to the tree whole night, his body was aching badly. His feet and wrists had swelled. The robbers, far from offering food, had not even given him a single drop of water throughout the night.

"Panditji! Gangaram has not yet returned; and now the only alternative we have, is to kill you and go in search of some other prey," Madhosing, the chief of robbers said.

"Mangalsingh! kill this Brahmin."

"As you wish, chief," saying this Mangalsingh pulled his sword out of the sheath and raised it.

Panditji looked timidly at the shining sword, his heart in his mouth. He said nervously, "No, no Mangalsingh! Please don't kill me."

"Do you expect us to sit and worship you? We have wasted one whole night waiting for your Gangaram. You had sent him to arrange money for saving your life, and that swine, far from arranging money, has run away with my horse also," said Madhosingh angrily.

"He has not run away, Madhosingh! He will definitely come back."

"But Madhosingh cannot wait anymore," groaned Madhosingh, "Mangalsingh! You do your job, and rest of you—make your preparations to make a move from here."

"Look, Madhosingh!" said Panditji in a last bid to save his life, "I shall make you immensely rich if you spare my life."

"Why, Pandit? Do you think we are fools?"

"No, no, I am not telling a lie. You can trust me."

"Just listen to this fool! This guy has no money to pay my tax, and he says he will make me immensely rich."

"What I am saying is true, Madhosingh."

"Shut up!"

"At least, give me a chance."

"Mangalsingh! You do your job."

"Chief!" said Mangalsingh, "We can kill this fool any time, but there is no harm in giving him a chance to prove his words."

"All right! In that case you listen to this fool; I have no patience."

"Look, Chief!" I have commanded a Mantra with the help of which

106

I can make diamonds and pearls pour in heaps. I shall have to utter this Mantra one thousand times."

"Why didn't you tell me earlier, if that was so? That means you want to cheat me."

"Madhosingh! what shall I get by cheating you?"

"Then why didn't you tell me earlier?"

"I didn't tell you because I wanted to extend the benefits of this Mantra to the king and please him, so that I could attain some high post in his court and pass the rest of my life comfortably."

"Why didn't you make use of this Mantra for your own personal gains?"

"Look, Madhosingh! I cannot use this Mantra to serve my personal ends. I shall die the moment I try to use it for myself."

"Give him a chance, chief. There may be some truth in what he is saying."

"All right! Pandit! I am giving you one last chance. If there is a rain of diamonds and pearls, I shall not only spare your life, I shall also arrange to see you off safely out of the borders of this forest. Tell me, what shall I have to do for this?"

"You shall have to free me first, and allow me to take bath in order to clean myself before I start my worship. And you will see, as soon as I finish uttering the Mantra one thousand times, diamonds and pearls will start pouring in. After that you go your way with all the diamonds and pearls and I shall go my way."

"All right!"

And with the permission of Madhosingh, Panditji was freed. Panditji went to take bath under the surveillance of two robbers. He returned after bath, sat under a tree and began uttering the Mantra.

Panditji was surrounded by curious robbers. Madhosingh was sitting alone in a corner. The eyes of all the robbers were fixed at Panditji. Sometimes they would start looking at the sky also, expecting some miracle to happen.

And then—

As soon as Pandittji had completed uttering the Mantra one thousand times, there really was a miracle.

A heavy rain of diamonds and pearls began.

"That's great, chief!" All the robbers went mad with happiness. "This is a miracle!"

Madhosingh was watching the miracle wide-eyed. He could not believe his eyes.

"Collect all the diamonds and pearls. This Pandit is true to his word. There really is great power in his Mantra. Ha, ha, ha! Pandit! You really have performed a miracle."

Diamonds and pearls rained for two minutes, and then everything became normal.

There was a big heap of diamonds and pearls before Madhosingh.

"Indeed you are great, Pandit! You have done a wonderful job. Now you can go; I free you."

Panditji had hardly gone a few steps from his place when again the forest was filled up with the sound of horse's hooves. Madhosingh and other robbers too heard this sound. They began looking at each other with surprise.

They heard a loud and harsh voice before they could understand anything.

"All of you, stay where you are! Don't move! Anyone trying to move will be killed."

Everyone was startled to hear someone roaring like a lion.

"Who is it!" roared Madhosingh. "Come out of your hiding and show your face. Who is there on earth who can challenge Madhosingh."

"Only a lion can challenge a lion, Madhosingh." A horseman appeared from behind the bushes. He had his friends behind him.

"How did you dare trespass on my land, Malkhan singh? Don't you know that you have crossed the borders of my area?"

"Only cowards care for demarcation of borders. I am the king of the whole forest. Now listen to me and do as I say. Don't try to be clever; all of you have been surrounded by us."

"That means you want bloodshed."

"It's upto you to interpret in any manner you like, Madhosingh. But remember one thing—There will be rivers of blood if I raised my sword. And I hate unnecessary bloodshed."

"Then why is it that you have come here?"

"I have come here for equity and justice."

"Equity and justice! Ha, ha, ha! Madhosingh began laughing. "Listen! Malkhansingh wants equity and justice. Ha, ha, ha."

Madhosingh's friends also began laughing loudly.

"Shut up!" shouted Malkhansingh. "Swine! You are laughing like a shameless person. You have tortured a Brahmin. It's a matter of shame for you, Madhosingh. You are a lineal descendant of Kshatriyas. And a Kshatriya is not supposed to oppress Brahmins."

"Stop talking nonsense and go your way. Either be prepared to face the consequences, or tell me the purpose of your visit."

"I have come here to have my share."

"Share! What Share?"

"I have heard there has been a rain of diamonds and pearls here. My logic is that if we share sun and cloud, rain and storm together equally, we must share diamonds and pearls also, that have fallen from the sky. Now I don't want you to make a fuss over this issue; be fair and give half of it in my share. You cannot take away such a big treasure alone. It will be good for both of us if we share it agreeably."

"Look, Malkhansingh! We both are robbers; and fighting together doesn't suit our profession. If you want, I can tell you the source of this treasure."

"If that is so, I shall myself go and take possession of the treasure. You only have to tell me where it is."

"But then you shall have to make a promise that you won't ask for a share from my lot."

"I am always true to my word. I am a real Kshatriya and I pay due respect to saints and Brahmins. Giving charities to them is a routine thing for me."

"Listen, Malkhan! this is Pandit Chandradatta. He has mastered a Mantra, the repetition of which causes diamonds and pearls to rain in heaps. It is this man who has caused this treasure to come down pouring in the form of rain," said Madhosingh. "So, stop quarrelling with me, and take this Pandit with yourself. Make use of him and he will make you so rich that even a king's treasure will not be able to match with your treasure."

"Is it true, Madhosingh?"

"You may ask my friends, if you don't trust me. Malkhan! It is true we are professional rivals today; but there was a time when we were very good friends. Forget our professional rivalry and trust me like a friend."

"What our chief is saying is true, Malkhansingh."

Madhosingh's friends' versions convinced Malkhansingh. "You have made our old friendship live again," said Malkhansingh in emotional tone. "Take hold of this Pandit, my friends. Now he will make diamonds and pearls rain for us."

Panditji was quick to understand that he was going to be in deep trouble. He had made a grave mistake by telling these robbers about Vaidarbha Mantra. He had thought that he would be able to save his life with the help of this Mantra, and now, it was this Mantra which was going to ruin his life.

He had almost managed to escape from the clutches of one robber, but the situation was such that he was going to fall in the hands of another robber.

"This means I am going from frying pan into the fire. Now these greedy idiots won't spare my life."

"O God! Strange are your ways. A learned Brahmin is in such a mess. Now there is total risk of life in the clutches of these demons. God! Have mercy on me; please save my life. The Mantra that I have mastered is effective only once in a year. this robber is sure to compel me to extend the benefits of this Mantra to him also; and I shall fail for the reason that it cannot produce results more than once in a year. This situation will become detrimental to my life. I am in a very strange state of predicament; O God! Please help me save my life. I should, alas, have listened to my protege and not told anything about the Vaidarbha Mantra to these robbers. God! Please save my life; get me out of this mess."

Panditji was muttering his prayers. Suddenly Malkhansingh roared, "O Pandit! What are you thinking? Read your Mantra one thousand times for me also and make the miracle happen before my eyes."

"Look, Malkhansingh!..."

Panditji had wanted to say something when Malkhansingh roared again, "No ifs and buts! I am not ready to hear any excuses. Do as I say, if you want safety of your life, or else your head won't remain on your shoulders."

"No, no, Malkhansingh! don't do that; kiling a Brahmin is the greatest sin.

"Don't try to define sin before me," groaned Malkhansingh and caught him by his neck, "or else, I shall strangle you to death."

"Please spare my life, Malkhansingh; listen to me first; my Mantra is effective only once in a year. I have already extended the benefits of this Mantra to Madhosingh. I promise, I shall do it for you next year."

"Stop talking nonsense, Pandit! A Mantra is effective any time you read it."

"But this Mantra is different."

"Now will you keep your trap shut? I have had enough of your nonsense."

"Please trust me, Malkhansingh."

"This means, I shall have to apply force on you." Saying this Malkhansingh began beating him severely, showering slaps and blows.

"Oh, oh, Malkhansingh! This is too rough a behaviour; this will kill me."

"All right, then! Tell me whether you will read the Mantra for me or not?"

"No!"

"Then, take it." Malkhansingh once again began showering blows on Panditji.

"Don't hit me, you sinner. Insulting a Brahmin will bring bad results. You shall never be happy."

Panditji continued screaming, but Malkhansingh didn't stop. He beat him so severely, that his teeth broke and he began bleeding from his mouth. After some time Panditiji fell unconscious.

"Water!" Mumbled Panditji in a feeble tone.

"Pandit! You will get water only after you make diamonds and pearls rain."

"Have mercy on me, Malkhan! Get me some water please...

"No, you won't get water."

Panditji's breathing became irregular. It became dark before his eyes. His heart began sinking; his hands and feet becoming loose; he looked up languidly and spoke whining with pain, "Remember, Malkhansingh! I am dying now, but you shall have to face bitter consequences. God will definitely punish you for your bad deeds."

Panditji breathed his last and left for his heavenly abode.

When Madhosingh saw Panditji dying, he signalled to his friends to stuff all the treasure in bags and sneak off silently. He knew, as soon as Malkhansingh realised that Panditji was dead, he would go mad with anger. 'Defeat' was not a word in his dictionary.

"Bring this Pandit to consciousness. It's all a farce," said Malkhan—singh.

His friends immediately rushed towards Panditji.

"He is dead, chief."

"What! He is dead?"

"Yes, chief."

"Oh, so much labour and no gain...and this swine—Madhosingh—has disappeared with all the treasure. Go, all of you; catch him; don't let him escape."

Next moment all his friends mounted their horses and rushed in the direction in which Madhosingh and other robbers had gone.

Madhosingh and his friends were being chased by Malkhansingh and his friends. The whole of the forest was resounding with the sound of the horses hooves.

When Madhosingh and his friends saw them coming behind, they clapped their spurs to the horses' flanks, and the horses began running much faster.

"Get them. Don't let them escape," shouted Malkhansingh, and they too sped their horses.

This running and chasing didn't continue for long.

Soon Malkhansingh and his friends got hold of Madhosingh and his friends.

And then—

The gory details of brutality went beyond description. The scene of bloody fight between two blood thirsty groups was ghastly. There was bloodshed all around. None of the two groups was weaker than the other. They were falling heavily upon each other.

Within moments the battle ground had become red with blood.

Both the chiefs were encouraging their friends to fight for victory. But how long could this ghastly fight continue? Soon all the robbers execpt Madhosingh and Malkhansihg were killed.

"Madhosingh! Get ready to die now," said Malkhansingh to Madhosingh, challenging him for a dual, brandishing a sword in his hand.

"Listen Malkhansingh!" said Madhosingh clinging to a clever ruse, "All our friends have been killed; if we too die fighting with each other, this treasure will be rendered meaningless. It is better if we divide it into two halves. It's still not too late."

"No. Either you kill me and take away this treasure, or I shall kill you and take this treasure away. I would have accepted your proposal of dividing it into two halves, if you had agreed on this point before all our friends had beed killed. No, no, your condition is not acceptable to me now. I neither fear death, nor am I weaker than you."

"Don't talk like mad, Malkhansingh. Here is not the question of weak or strong. Look at our friends! What could they take with them? Why should there be a fight if a person cannot take away anything from here to the other world? The wisest thing would be to divide this treasure into two halves and pass the rest of our lives comfortably like good friends. If we have wealth, we can form new bands of robbers.

Malkhansingh's eyelids crinkled at the outer corners of his eyes, giving a thoughtful gesture. He felt that Madhosingh was correct in a way. He could understand that dying for no fruitful reasons was unwise.

"All right! Madhosingh! I accept your proposal." Saying this Malkhansingh threw away his sword.

They embraced each other.

"Madhosingh! We are renewing our friendship today."

"Yes, let us promise that we shall remain united for ever from today."

"I promise," said Malkhansingh, then after thinking for a while, he again said, "but I have to give you an advice, my friend."

"What is it?"

"I think it is not advisable to carry such a big treasure always with us."

"Then..."

"It would be better if we hide it somewhere and take out little by little as and when required."

"What you say is correct and bears some sense. All right let us do it."

If two parties agree on a common point, it doesn't take time to bring shape to the plan. Both were powerful and courageous. They dug a pit under a big Peepal tree and buried the bags of treasure in it.

Having finished this task, Madhosingh said, "Malkhan! The job is over what shall we do now?"

"You suggest."

"First we shall have to manage some meals; I am feeling terribly hungry. But where shall we get food in this forest?

"I too am feeling hungry. Let us go to the town where we shall eat to our hearts' content. But, friend! Will it be wise to leave such a big treasure unguarded here? At least one of us should remain here to guard it.

"I agree with you friend. Let us do one thing—one of us will remain here, and the other one will go to town to bring food. All right! You stay here and I shall go to town to bring some food. But let us swear in the name of goddess Durga that none of us will cheat the other."

"Yes, I swear in the name of goddess Durga that we shall not cheat each other."

And then Madhosingh went to town to bring food.

Malkhansingh was left alone. His eyes were shining with cunningness. Though he had sworn in the name of goddess Durga, he already had plans in his mind to cheat Madhosingh. He began thinking—'I shall become the sole owner of this treasure, if I kill Madhosingh. Then I shall give up this nasty profession and live a comfortable life in the town. There is no harm in sacrificing one more life on the altar of this treasure. Once Madhosingh is killed, the whole treasure will become mine.'

Thinking this Malkhansingh laughed.

On the other side, Madhosingh was advancing towards the town in great speed. He reached the town after some time. While returning to the forest, a thought arose in his mind—'Malkhansingh is very clever and cunning. Though he has established friendship with me in the name of goddess Durga, he is sure to cheat me one day or the other. Why not kill him and get rid of him once for ever. And then the whole of the treasure will be mine, and I shall settle down in the town and live a comfortable and luxurious life.'

Thinking this he bought some poison from a shop and mixed it with the food.

Nature has its own ways of settling its score with the people on the earth. Strangely Malkhansingh and Madhosingh both had finalised their plans to kill each other.

Malkhansingh was sitting with his sword in his hand near the buried treasure, waiting for Madhosingh. Just then, seeing Madhosingh coming at a distance, he hid himself behing the tree. He had decided to let Madhosingh come within range and then cut his throat off with a whack of his sword.

And this is what happened.

As soon as Madhosingh came within range, Malkhansingh came out from behind the tree and cut his head off with one powerful blow of his sword.

"Ha, ha, ha!" Malkhansingh gave a loud boisterous laugh at his success. "Now all this treasure is mine. I have become a king. I am no more Malkhansingh—the robber. I am king Malkhansingh. O trees and plants! Say—'Victory to king Malkhansingh'. Ha, ha, ha."

Having killed his rival Malkhansingh twirled his moustaches. Just then his eyes fell on the packet of food. He was already hungry, and seeing the food-packet before him, he began feeling ten times more hungry. He rushed at the food and began eating hurriedly.

One morsel of food had gone down his throat, and his eyes popped out. He began frothing at his mouth and within moments, he was dead.

All had died and there was none to claim the treasure buried under the Peepal tree.

❑ ❑

9

HONOURED BY A RAM

A strange fair used to be organised every year in Vijayapur state. It was strange because it used to be a fair of rams. The villagers of the neighbouring villages used to collect in the fair with their stout rams, arrange a fight between two rams and enjoy the scene.

This year also a fair of rams had been organised. There was a big crowd of thousands in the main market of the town. So, many farmers had brought at least one stout ram each with them. Just as a fight of rams was going to be organised, a saint happened to arrive at that place, and seeing a big gathering he enquired about the occasion and the reason behind such a big gathering.

One of the farmers explained to him—"Maharaj! this is a fair of rams, and it is organised here every year. So many groups of two rams each is made and they are made to fight between them. The winning ram in the finals is declared the king of rams, and the owner of the winning ram is awarded lots of prizes."

"Is that so?" said the saint with surprise and making his way through the crowd. He came forward and stood right before the arena to have a clearer view.

The fight had started and everyone was watching it with great interest. Suddenly one of the fighting rams stopped and began looking at the saint with his gaze fixed on him. The other ram also stopped.

The ram came and stood before the saint. It recoiled a few paces with its head down, ready to charge at him.

But the saint thought, "Ah, here is a good and intelligent animal. He has realised that I am a man of merit, and he is bowing to give me a salute. At least he knows how to honour a saint."

The owner of the ram was quick to realise that the saint was feeling flattered, so in a bid to alert him, he said, "Maharaj! Please get out of its way or else it will hit you. Don't think that this ram in bowing before you in a gesture of salute; it is preparing itself to launch an attack on you. Be careful, please!"

"No, no, come on! This is a spechless creature. How will it hit anyone. It, in fact, wants to have my blessings. It is us human beings who torture these spechless creature."

"Maharaj! You are forgetting that it's a ram and is violent by nature. Even God cannot change its nature. It is the individual nature of every creature in the world that tells about it."

"No, no, you are a fool!"

Another person standing near him, said, "Maharaj! These rams are meant for fighting. Violence is there in their nature."

But the saint didn't listen to anyone. On the contrary, he advanced towards the ram.

And the ram also advanced two paces towards the saint. The owner of the ram tried to stop the ram, but by that time it was too late.

And in the twinkling of an eye, the ram took the saint on its horns and sent him rolling to the ground.

"Hey, Ram!" The saint shrieked with pain.

The saint fell face down on the ground and broke all his teeth. His mouth filled with blood.

People around somehow managed to push the ram back and helping the saint stand on his feet, they said, "Why, Maharaj! Had we not told you that rams are violent by nature?"

"Yes, brothers!" said the saint whining with pain—"It was indeed my mistake. You were right when you said that rams are violent by nature. Oh, God! It has broken my bones."

Poeple pulled the saint back and gave him some water to clean his mouth. The saint took water in his mouth and kept squirting it out until his mouth became clean. Then he was offered some milk to drink. Now it had become clear to the saint that every creature has its own individual nature.

❑ ❑

10

DECIDING THE SHARE

THERE lived a pair of male and female jackals in a forest. They loved each other very much. The male jackal loved the female jackal so much that he would fulfil every demand made by her. One day the female jackal said, "Dear! I have a great urge for eating fish today."

"That's no problem. I shall bring fish for you, if you have an urge for it, dear."

Saying this he set out in search of fish.

While going towards the river, he began thinking—'I have promised my wife to arrange fish for her, but I know nothing about fishing. How to fulfil my wife's demand for fish?'

Lost in these thoughts the jackal reached the bank of the river and sitting in a corner he began looking at the frolicking fish with greedy eyes. For once he felt like jumping into the river and getting the required fish in the twinkling of an eye. But seeing water all around in the big river, and the water current, frightened him. He got so scared to see the vast river that he went away from the river-bank and sat under a tree at quite a distance. He began thinking of some possible ruse to get the fish without risking his life.

Just then he saw an otter bringing a big fish out of the river with the help of his friends.

One otter said to the other—"This is a very big fish. We can manage our meals with this fish for days together."

"Yes, brother! This is after a very long time that we have fished such a big one."

"The jackal's mouth began watering to see that fish. He began thinking of ways to manage to get the fish from their possession.

He thought—'Using my wits I can manage to get the fish in my possession.'

The otters somehow pulled the fish to the bank of the river. One of the otters said, "Friend! we have got only one fish between us; and we are two. How to decide our shares!"

"Let us do it ourselves," said the other one.

"Look, brother!" said the first one, "Deciding the shares ourselves will give a rise to doubt in our minds, and both of us will keep thinking that the other one may have taken a larger share. So, this is my sincere advice that we get the shares decided by someone who is not one of us; a third one."

The jackal became very happy to hear this. He came forward like an elderly person and said, "Brother! What's your problem?"

"Not a big problem," said one otter, "In fact, we both of us have killed this big fish. We are two and we have got only one fish between us. Now the problem is how to decide our shares."

"This can be done by someone who is not one of us," said the other otter.

"What you say is correct, brother. Look, if you want I can help you. I take pleasure in solving the problems of others. If you wish I can bring out an amicable solution to your dispute."

"All right, brother! I have no objection, provided he too doesn't have any objections," said one otter.

"I too, have no objection, brother."

"That's great! This is called friendship. A peaceful agreement solves many big problems. We should always share our meals together; we must trust each other; there isn't anything greater than love and affection in this world. Both of you please wait for me here. I shall go and bring a knife from somewhere, so that it becomes easy to cut the fish and decide your shares."

"Yes, yes, brother! Please go and bring a knife. We shall wait for you here."

While coming towards the river, the jackal had seen a farmer lying in his cot and guarding his farm. He had also seen a wooden staff and a big knife on his cot. The farmer was sleeping when the jackal reached there. He quietly picked up the knife and returned with it.

Both the otters saw him returning with a big knife happily.

"Come brothers! Now I can help you solve your problem."

Saying this the jackal cut the fish into three pieces. First he cut the head off and then the tail.

"Brother! You take the top portion of the fish—the head; and you take the bottom portion—the tail."

Both took their shares, and now they had their eyes fixed on the middle portion of the fish. Both were thinking that the jackal would divide the middle portion also into two halves and give them their shares.

But the jackal took the third piece in his possession.

"Brother! Will you not divide the remaining piece and give us our shares?"

"This piece should not concern you, brother," said the jackal looking at them with angry eyes. "This is for the job done by me. Will you not pay me for the pains taken by me in going all the way to get a knife and decide your shares for you? The fruits of hard work should be shared by all. After all I too am your friend.

Saying this the jackal took the middle portion of the fish in his mouth and went away. Both the otters were left behind to see him go with the largest of the three pieces of the fish. And by the time they realised what had actually happened, it was too late.

"Brother! How much better it would have been, if we had decided our shares ourselves. Now see! He gave us the top and the bottom portions of the fish in our shares and went away with the largest piece in his mouth."

The other otter said, "Someone has correctly said that a dispute between two friends always benefits the third one. Now let us take a lesson from this event that a marginal difference in our share would not bother us, and we shall never allow anyone to mediate between us."

❏ ❏

11

PUNISHMENT TO A GREEDY CROW

SETH Ram Lal was a famous businessman. He was very rich and there was no shortage of any kind in his house. There was not a single day in the month when he did not entertain guests, and that too in the most lavish manner.

There was a pigeon who had made a nest in the kitchen of Seth Ram Lal's house, and lived there.

The pigeon was simple and gentle.

The cook—Shambhoo Maharaj—who worked in Seth Ram Lal's kitchen, liked the pigeon very much. While cooking, the cook would put some food near the nest, and the pigeon would peck at it and fly away. It would come back and sleep cosily in his nest in the evening.

Thus, the pigeon was passing its life comfortably and peacefully.

One day while the pigeon was relaxing after having his meals, a crow happened to pass by.

He became very happy to see a pigeon sitting at the ventilator of the kitchen. There was a sweet cooking smell coming from the kitchen.

"Ah! What a nice smell! I can also see nest of a pigeon in the kitchen." The crow alighted on a branch of a tree in front of the house and began thinking—'This pigeon has nested in the very kitchen of Ram Lal Seth's house. It must be getting very nice preparations to eat. I must make friends with this pigeon. And once I make friends with him, I too shall get nice things to eat. O God! This kind of food is beyond imagination for me.'

Thinking this the crow began waiting for the pigeon to come out. His greedy eyes were fixed on the dainty dishes kept in the kitchen.

After some time when the pigeon came out for fresh air, the crow also began flying after it.

When the pigeon realised after some time that the crow was continuously following him, the pigeon thought—"Why is this crow following me? These are very cunning type of creatures."

The crow was still flying after the pigeon.

At last the pigeon got irritated and asked—"Brother! Why is it that you have been following me?"

Hearing the pigeon the crow laughed and said, "Brother! You are a gentle and virtuous creature. There is none among us birds who could be considered so virtuous and innocent. And this pricisely is the reason why I wish to make friends with you."

"We are temperamentally different. How can we have friendship? I am simple and vegetarian, and you are clever and carnivorous."

"Dear brother! A creature eating flesh doesn't necessarily have to be bad. And so far as being simple or clever is concerned, let me tell you that all the five fingers are not equal in size. You can find clever and wicked creatures in every class, and giving bad name to a whole class because of one is not justifiable."

"No, no, brother! Make friends with someone else."

"Look, brother! We are the creatures who are disliked by everyone; we are also considered foolish—a creature without brain. Will you also say no to my friendship? At least, if you allow me your company, I too shall attain some wisdom." While saying so the crow pretended as if he was on the verge of weeping.

The pigeon was moved to see him so sad and said, "But, brother crow! How can we live together? We are poles apart in looks and behaviour. There is no similarity between me and you."

"O brother! That similarity will come gradually and automatically. I shall change my food habits, and start eating what you eat; I shall change my behaviour also. Haven't you heard that even the wretched ones change in the company of good ones? The philosopher's stone transmutes base metals into gold."

"Brother! We shall live together if you insist so much. It is generally said that it is better to be in someone's company than being a recluse. But, brother! Please see that you don't do any mischief. Because any act of mischief will deprive us of our dwelling place."

"Oh no, brother! Why should I do any such thing? I am aware that doing any such thing will not be in my favour. I am also aware that any kind of mischief will deprive me of your kind company also."

"All right! come with me."

The crow was very happy at his success in making a successful beginning.

Whole day they kept pecking at grains and talking to each other. The crow was very talkative, and the pigeon was a good listener. All day the crow kept telling him stories about himself, trying to impress upon him that he was the only well-wisher and friend of the pigeon.

The pigeon was slightly impressed by the crow.

In the evening both flew back to their dwelling place.

Once again the pigeon warned the crow and said, "Brother! Please be careful and see to it that you don't do anything that may prove to be detrimental to us. This is for the last time that I am alerting you."

"O my brother!" said the crow, "Don't put me to shame by telling me the same thing again and again.

"But, yes...!" As if the pigeon remembered something. He said, "I have got only one nest in the kitchen I live in. How shall we live together?"

"It hardly matters, brother! We shall somehow manage in the same nest tonight; and tomorrow—though it's a hard task for me—I shall make a separate nest for myself. And once we two friends start making a nest together, it won't take much time."

Poor pigeon was left speechless. The crow was coming out with logical solutions to every problem discussed by him. At last the pigeon thought it better to keep silent.

There was no danger to the pigeon from cook's side. He knew, the cook was very kind-hearted. He will consider my friendship with the crow and allow him also some place in the kitchen. He already has great love for birds.

Now the problem of stay was over, and the crow considered it his second success.

That night, the crow also got pulse fried in butter, rice, and vegetable etc. to eat. Cooked meals, that too fried in butter, was something beyond his imagination. He ate everything with great relish. That night he slept completely relaxed in the nest of the pigeon.

Next day the crow also built a nest in a corner of the kitchen with the help of the pigeon. When the cook saw a nest of a crow also in the kitchen, he became very happy thinking that at least the pigeon wouldn't feel isolated and will enjoy someone's company. But then he thought that crows are cunning and mischievous by nature. One day he might cause great harm to this pigeon.

The crow was very happy; he was enjoying new kinds of dishes every day. He was living in luxury now.

One day—

Seth Ram Lal had invited some distinguished guests. Various kinds of dainty dishes were being prepared in their honour. One of the items to be cooked for the guests was fish.

While the cook was cleaning the fish, the crow sitting in his nest was thinking—'O God! this is great! I shall be getting fried fish to eat today after a very long time.'

The crow, sitting quietly in his nest, was thinking of some possible way to manage to get a few pieces of fish. He thought if he discussed the matter with the pigeon, he wouldn't allow him to take even a single piece of it. So, it would be better if he managed it himself.

It was morning, and the pigeon, as usual, told the crow to set out with him in search of food.

But the crow had some other plans. He said, "No, dear! somehow I am not feeling well today. My stomach is not in order since yesterday."

The crow considered himself very intelligent, but the pigeon was no less intelligent. It didn't take him time to understand that it was the fish in the kitchen which was holding him back; the crow was making only lame excuses. So, he said, "Look, brother! No wrong activity in the kitchen, please. Don't touch anything or else we both will be in great trouble. Please listen to me and come with me."

"Oh no, dear! I am not telling a lie. Please don't think that it's the fish which is holding me back and I am making false excuses. Please believe me; my stomach is upset and I am not in a position to go out."

"All right! Then in that case I am going alone; but, before I leave, I must alert you once again not to indulge into any kind of activity that may tell upon us."

"You can trust me, brother."

The crow's repeated assurances had a positive effect on the pigeon and he believed that the crow wouldn't do anything wrong.

Poor pigeon went out in search of food for himself.

"Now this hindrance has also been cleared," thought the crow to himself. "How a pigeon can understand the taste of fish? Anyway...now I am free to eat and enjoy."

Not much after, the cook came in the kitchen and began filleting the fish; brushed the fillets with the marinade and left it to marinate, so that it could develop special flavour. After some time he fried the pieces in butter. Having done this, he cut the vegetables also and cleaned them.

All this tired the cook so much that he went out of the kitchen to relax.

'Thank God! This cook has at least moved out of the kitchen. Had he remained sitting in the kitchen, it wouldn't have been possible for me to get even a single piece. Already it was with great difficulty that I managed to send the pigeon away from here.

And then the crow came down, stole a piece of fish from the basket, took it to his nest and began eating it quietly.

Thus, he took away many pieces one by one and ate them stealthily.

Though he was fully satiated now, it was his greed that kept pressing him to go in for more of them. And greed is something that always brings sad ends.

And that's exactly what happened.

This time, as soon as he picked up a piece of fish, the shallow large dish of brass, with which the basket was partially covered, tumbled down producing a lot of harsh metallic sound.

It of course didn't make any difference to the crow; he quietly took one more piece to his nest and began eating it. But the cook became alert and he rushed in, thinking that some cat might have entered the kitchen. As soon as the cook saw the crow eating fish, he became terribly angry.

He rushed at the crow in great anger—"You wretched bird! Is this the way you could have repaid my gentleness? It was becuase of the pigeon that I allowed you to stay here; but now since you have stooped down to this ruse to serve your selfish ends, you will get what you rightly deserve.

Saying this he caught the crow by his neck and stripped him off his feathers in a sudden paroxysm of anger. The crow kept screaming with pain but his shrieks and screams could not strike a responsive chord in the heart of the cook.

"Now rot here, you greedy crow! This is your punishment.

Shocked with fear and whining with pain, the crow lay sitting in a corner; and now he was shedding tears of repentance. In the evening, when the pigeon returned, he saw the pitiable condition of the crow, and he immediately understood that the crow must have been punished for his misdeed.

"Why, brother crow! Had I not warned you against any wrong doing? Had I not told you to exercise check on your instincts? One should be content with whatever little one gets. But you didn't listen to me. Your greediness caused you to irritate the cook to such an extent that the always kind cook also could not control his anger, and brought you to this end. It is rightly said that greed is the worst of all evils.

❑ ❑

12

VANITY OF KALINGRAJ

KALINGA was under the reign of a very powerful and brave king, a few thousand years ago. He had a very powerful army with four divisions. Coming to know any king's power and might used to fill him with jealousy. He would create a deliberate rift with the king, wage a war against him, kill his pride and then only his vanity would be assuaged. This caused great fear in the hearts of all the kings on the earth. Some kings who refused to surrender before him without a fight were defeated by him, and some accepted their defeat without getting into war. Thus, not only that all the kings surrendered to his might, but they also declared him the bravest of all.

Thus, it was a long time since he had not fought with any king; and who to fight with; no king had courage enough to fight against his large and powerful army. And for the king of Kalinga, not a single moment without war was acceptable to him. War was his hobby, his life; he was addicted to it. But every time the question remained unanswered—'Fight with whom?'

It is said—'The more one becomes powerful, the more his ambitions grow.' There is no end to ambitions. And this exactly was the problem of Kalingraj.

Despite being so powerful he had a hankering for becoming more and more powerful. There was a vanity in him that would be satisfied by crushing someone's legitimate pride only. He used to be mighty pleased to see a defeated king bowing before him. And this was something that had not happened for a long time.

And also this precisely was the reason why Kalingraj was feeling uneasy. He sent his spies in all the four directions to find out if he was being criticized anywhere or if there was any king hatching a conspiracy against him. He wanted every such information that could enable him to find some excuse to wage a war against such a king.

The spies spread around without caring for storm or sun; but they had to return soon, as they could neither find anyone criticizing him, nor was there any king conspiring against him.

Kalingraj was greatly disappointed to hear this. He had every happiness and prosperity in his kingdom, but all this could not please him. He was not satisfied.

At last when his uneasiness reached its height, he called a meeting of his ministers and said, "Ministers! Sitting idle thus has bored me stiff. I want war. But there is none to accept it; no king is prepared to fight with me. Can't anyone of you find some way so that I get a chance to declare war against someone?"

"My Lord!" The chief minister said, "There should be some legitimate reason to declare war against someone; but here the position is that even the kings of far off countries have surrendered before your might—what to talk of the kings of neibhouring countries.

Even your name is enough to make someone bow down. Diplomacy says that fighting against those who have already surrendered before you, or against those who give due recognition to your might, is not justifiable. This will not only lower your status, it will also bring bad name to you."

"Then you yourself suggest some way to me. I am feeling ill at ease with this kind of situation; life without war has no meaning for me, and you say that it is unethical to declare war against someone without assigning any justifiable reasons." Kalingraj sopke despondently, "How will my wish be fulfilled after all; how long it has been since I have not fought a battle? How long shall I sit idle? Can't all of you create some reason for war?"

"My Lord! There is one ruse we have to cling to in order to create circumstances for war," said one of the ministers.

"Minister! What is it? Tell me immediately."

"My Lord! Your daughters are breathtakingly beautiful. There are so many big kings who have immense desire to marry your daughters and form relationship with you. But it is because of the fear of your might that no king has dared express his wish. So, please send the princesses in a chariot, covered from all sides, to every kingdom, and also let the charioteer be accompanied by a person who will keep announcing that anyone who is man enough could marry the princesses subject to the condition that he will have to prove his manliness by agreeing to fight with Kalingraj. I believe this allurement will work and some foolish king will agree to accept your challenge."

"Oh, that's great. This is a very good scheme. This will save me from being blamed for challenging a weak king and fighting with him and my wish for war will also be fulfilled." Kalingraj became extremely happy. He said, "Chief minister! Send the princesses on a country-wide tour tomorrow itself."

And then, on the very next day, the princesses were made to make a move with certain important officials of the court followed by a division of army. They would make the announcement but none would dare take the challenge. After all one needed guts to accept the challenge of Kalingraj and there was almost none gutsy enough to accept it.

Having taken a complete round of Jamboodweep, the chariot began advancing towards Assak kingdom. The king of Assak had already been infromed about this by his spies. So, before the chariot could enter the town, he sent gifts in the honour of Kalingraj, got all the gates of the town closed and took a sigh of relief. Sending gifts and getting the gates of the town closed under trepidation was something not acceptable to Nandisen—the minister of the king of Assak. And the challenging announcements made by the officials of Kalingraj had distrubed him all the more.

He said to the king of Assak, "My Lord! It is more praiseworthy to die fighting in the battlefield and attain martyrdom, than to live with a blame of unmanliness. It's my humble suggestion that you please invite the princesses to your kingdom with due honour and accept the challenge of Kalingraj, so that he realises that the land of Assaks is not devoid of brave people. If we win, the whole world will be full of priase for you; if we lose, at least we shall be called men of self-respect. Losing a battle is a different thing, but returning the princesses set out in search of their suitors is a matter of insult."

The king was very much impressed to hear his minister. He immediately ordered the gates of the town to open and invited the princesses to his palace with due honour and respect. And then he sent his messengers to Kalingraj to inform him of his acceptence of challenge thrown by him.

Kalingraj was already awaiting such an opportunity. So he set out with his four-divisioned army as soon as he got the news.

He reached the borders of Assak kingdom with his large army. Nandisen sent his messenger to Kalingraj with a proposal that the armies of both the kingdoms should restrict themselves within their border areas and the battle should be fought in the battlefield which is between the border areas of both the kingdoms. Kalingraj agreed to this proposal and ordered his army to halt.

There was a saint's hut near the battlefield. One day Kalingraj met him donned in disguise. He requested him to prophesy the results of the war waged by him. Though he was confident of his victory, he wanted to confirm it. The saint was unable to make any prophecy at that time. He asked Kalingraj to come on the next day. After he left, the saint, using his spiritual powers, contacted Lord Indra in the subtle world and asked—"Who will be the winner of the ensuing battle, and what will be the signs that will appear on the battlefield, observing which one could assure oneself of the prophecy made by you?"

Lord Indra drew a very clear picture of the battle and its results before the saint and evanesced. Next day again Kalingraj came to the saint to get an answer to his question. The saint remained indifferent and said, "This battle will be won by Kalingraj and lost by Assakraj."

Hearing this Kalingraj jumped with happiness. He didn't wait another minute and returned without asking any other question. As soon as he reached his camp, he announced the prophecy made by the saint before his army; and there was a great jubilation all around. There was a great rejoicing among his army generals. Gradually the prophecy made by the saint, reached the ears of Assakraj also. He was already frightened, and coming to know of the prophecy made by the saint, left him half dead.

Though Assakraj was losing his confidence, his minister was not the one who would lose his courage so soon. He had a firm determination that no matter what, Kalingraj has got to be defeated this time. In order to check the truth in the rumour spread by Kalingraj, Nandisen himself went to see the saint in the night. The saint told him also the same thing. The minister asked again, "Maharaj! what will be the auspicious and inauspicious signs visible to the winners and losers of the war?"

The saint said, "Assakraj will see a white bullock with the army of Kalingraj. He will be the Guardian Angel of Kalingraj; and Kalingraj will see a bullock with the army of Assakraj, which will represent the god of death."

Nandisen returned from there. He was not in the least disappointed to hear the prophecy. He selected one thousand soldiers of proven capability. He tested them in many ways to see what they could do for their king. Having tested them in many ways, Nandisen was satisfied; he said, "Now I am convinced that none of you will hesitate to sacrifice your life if it came to that. All of you are expected to fight with the enemy with this very spirit."

War began on due date. Since Kalingraj had full faith in the prophecy made by the saint and had taken his victory for granted, he didn't make any special efforts to win the war. Whereas Assakraj was fighting the battle with all his might in self-defence. At times Nandisen noticed Assakraj losing his confidence, and like a loyal minister he came from behind and exhorted him to fight the battle with great vigour. He himself was fighting with all his power. Despite all this Assakraj was not able to make the enemy retreat. Just then Nandisen remembered the prophecy of the saint. He immediately turned to Assakraj and asked, "Maharaj! Do you see some animal on the side of your enemy?" The king said, "Yes! I see a white bullock on their side."

Nandisen immediately brought the one thousand chosen soldiers forward and said, "Maharaj! Please advance with these soldiers; go and kill that bullock. It is because of that bullock that Kalingraj has remained invincible despite every efforts made by us. First kill the bullock and then take on the enemy.

Assakraj began advancing with his one thousand chosen soldiers, facing the enemy bravely and killing a significant number of them. He reached the middle of the enemy's army. The soldiers of Kalingraj tried their level best to check the advancing army of one thousand fearless soldiers of Assakraj, but they couldn't. Those chosen soldiers were not ordinary ones. They were ready to sacrifice their lives for their king—Assakraj. Reaching there the king killed the bullock with one blow of his sword. Kalingraj's supernatural power was annihilated with the killing of the bullock.

This created so much confidence in Assakraj that he began slicing his enemy as if they were no match to his power. The enemy began running away from the battlefield in nervousness. Now Assakraj's enthusiasm knew no bounds. Things had taken a queer turn. Circumstances changed; Kalingraj was on the losing side now. His dreams of victory had shattered. He somehow managed to save his life, and escaped from the battlefield. While running away he saw the saint in the way. He said, "You cheat! I made the biggest mistake by believing in your prophecy. Had I not depended on your prophecy, I would have fought the war vigorously. And I would not have met this end."

Saying this he set out to his capital in great speed. On the other side the saint was greatly surprised to see the prophecy of Lord Indra proving false. He once again invoked Lord Indra in the night and said, "Lord! You had prophesied that Guardian Angel is in favour of Kalingraj and he will win the battle. But surprisingly it is Assakraj who won the battle. How did this happen?"

Lord Indra said, "God helps those who help themselves. The gods turned in favour of Assakraj seeing his self-control, patience, courage, enthusiasm, and valour. The time I made the prophecy, I was confident that Kalingraj would display his valour as he had done in earlier battles; but on the contrary, assured of his victory, he loosened his grip. Whereas Assakraj displayed valour beyond comparison. In the beginning the gods were against him, but later his brave performance in the battlefield enamoured them of him. They gave up the idea of causing evil to him, and thus he became successful."

Saying this Lord Indra evanesced. Assakraj returned to his palace with flying colours. On the suggestion of Nandisen, he sent a message to Kalingraj on the next day that he was going to marry his daughters and that Kalingraj should make necessary arrangements for his daughters' marriage, or else he would himself have to launch an attack on his kingdom and marry his daughters forcibly.

Kalingraj was no more a powerful king; he had no guts to refuse to fulfil any demand made by Assakraj. In order to satisfy Assakraj he had to give a very heavy dowry. But the positive side of all this was that he dared not enter into conflict with any king after that.

Someone has rightly said that he, who, lost in the pride of success, and stops making efforts to maintain it, is bound to meet the fate of Kalingraj.

❏ ❏

13

UNENDING LUST

THE king of Varanasi—Brahmdatt—had two sons. He had declared his elder son—the crown-prince—and the younger son—the commander-in-chief of his royal army. Brahmdatt died after some time. Under these circumstance the elder prince had the legitimate right to ascend the throne. So, the royal priest and the ministers began making preparations for the coronation of the elder prince; but the elder prince was far away from greed and lust of any kind, and also he had great affections for his younger brother. So, he declined to ascend the throne and declare himself a king. Out of affection he wanted to bestow this honour on his younger brother. Despite everyone's opposition he offered the throne to his younger brother. He had developed a kind of disinclination towards royal living and power. Now he wanted to lead a simple life; absolutely like an ordinary person.

He enthroned his younger brother and left the kingdom willingly. He went to a province which was at quite a distance from his kingdom, and began working in the house of a businessman.

Though he had kept his identity a secret, somehow the businessman came to know everything about him. From that day onwards his behaviour changed with him. The businessman became very alert and he took great care to see that the prince in disguise was not asked to do any work. Now his treatment with him was that would suit the status of a person of royal descent.

One day the elder prince came to know that the king's officials had come to the farms of the village and were taking measurements of farms afresh in order to enhance the taxes, and that the businessman was very much disturbed in view of enhancement of taxes. He took it to be his solemn duty to extend some help to his benefactor. He wrote a letter to the king—his younger brother—that he was living comfortably in the house of a businessman, and so the levy of tax may be foregone in favour of the businessman.

The younger brother gave due honour to his letter and ordered his officials to forego the tax in favour of the businessman.

The businessman became very happy when he came to know what great favour the prince had extended to him without letting him know anything about it. He brought it to the notice of others also in his village in order to impress upon others that a prince was living in his house. The result was that the people of the village and from nearby provinces rushed to the prince to have their taxes also foregone. As expected, the prince did not disappoint anyone. He wrote letters to the king for everyone and ultimately the king—his younger brother—withdrew his orders for levy of taxes in favour of everyone.

Now everyone in the village became an ardent admirer of the prince, and they seated him on the throne of king in their hearts. And thus, by his good deeds and kind-heartedness, he established complete sovereignty all over the province. The subjects of the province unanimously declared him a free king. Someone has correctly said— 'There is none in the world who, once given power, wouldn't be affected by vanity.' A person who once had given away his kingdom considering it worthless, was now gripped by the lust for power. He wrote to his younger brother in clear words—....'from now onwards, this province will be ruled by me only.' His younger happily accepted his demand. Even this did not satisfy him. He expressed his wish to take over the neighbouring provinces also. His younger brother accepted this demand also without any hesitation. All his demands were being met one by one, but there was no end to his always growing demands. Now he began making plans to occupy the whole kingdom.

He had doubts that his younger brother won't relinquish the throne so easily. So taking all the people of the provinces under his rule, he launched an attack on Varanasi.

He reached the gate of the palace with a big crowd. He sent a challenge from there to his brother—'Either relinquish the throne or face my army.'

His younger brother was in a strange state of predicament. He thought—'If I surrender, I shall be considered cowardly, and if i fight with his army and kill him, I shall earn a bad name and be accused of fratricide.' It was a difficult situation. He, after contemplating the matter for a long time, decided to hand over the throne to him. He brought him in with due honour and enthroned him.

Now the elder prince became the king of Varanasi. One by one all his desires were fulfilled; still there was no end to his greed and lust. Now the situation was that fulfilment of one desire gave rise to another desire, and then another desire. And then crossing all the bounds of desire, he began thinking of extending the territory of his country, and become an emperor. So, he began declaring war against the neighbouring kings and fighting with them. This had become his everyday routine. He could not bear to see the opulence of any prospering king. Day by day not only his tendencies were changing, but his lust for power was also growing to mesmerizing proportions.

Lord Indra became very sad to see his growing lust. On one auspicious day he went to the king donned in disguise of a Brahmachari*, and taking him in isolation he said, "Maharaj! I am coming after seeing three such provinces which are very prosperous and have boundless wealth. You can virtually see gold raining in every house. I would rather suggest to you to take those provinces in your possession and bring it under your rule.

Hearing this the king became impatient to attack those three provinces and take possession of as soon as possible. The Brahmachari quietly left the palace after conveying his message. The king didn't even care to know his name and address, because after hearing about the wealth and prosperity of those three provinces, he had lost his mental equilibrium. He called the ministers and said, "Just

* a person who vows to remain celibate throughout his life.

now I have been informed by a Brahmachari that there are three very opulent provinces somewhere. There is wealth beyond measure. I must get such remarkable provinces under my rule as soon as possible. Mobilize the army immeditely. I wish to capture the provinces brought to my notice by the Brahmachari, without delay."

The minister said, "Maharaj! Where are those provinces?"

The king was stunned to realise his mistake. He said, "I don't know; I forgot to enquire about their location. But the Brahmachari knows. He has seen those provinces with his own eyes. You go and ask him; he must be standing outside."

The minister went out in search of the Brahmachari, but he was not to be seen anywhere. He returned disappointed and said, "Maharaj! God knows where he has disappeared. I launched a massive search for him, but he has vanished without trace."

The king was shocked to hear this. He said, "O God! What will happen now? I was so selfish that I didn't talk to him any further on this topic. I forgot to extend due hospitality to him. He must have left out of anger. O God! Had I only asked him about the location of those provinces, I would have added three more provinces under my rule. Where to find that Brahmachari now? I forgot to enquire about his address also. How to get to him?"

Repenting thus the king became very sad. Day and night he would think of those three provinces only and keep cursing himself for not having enquired about their locations. This caused him to have sleepless nights and indigestion. Gradually his mental agony began affecting his stomach and thus he began suffering from acute diarrhoea. The best doctors of his kingdom administered the best possible medicines to him, but nothing worked; and that was solely because they had not been able to diagnose his problem correctly.

It was during those days that Bodhisatva had returned after completing his education in Ayurvedic science. He too came to know about the incurable disease of the king, and himself offered to render treatment to him. He sent a message to the king and began waiting for

his response at the palace gate.

The king was almost mad with stomach-ache, but he didn't want to consult an inexperienced doctor; and at the same time he also wanted to get rid of the problem. A drowning person is so muddle-headed that he would cling to a twig also in order to save his life. So he called the new doctor in and said, "Young man! All the experienced doctors of my kingdom have declared my disease incurable. Please don't take unnecessary pains; there is hardly any chance of my survival."

Bodhisatva listened to him patiently and said, "Maharaj! There isn't anything to be worried about. Even the incurable diseases become curable if diagnosed correctly. Please tell me how and when were you hit by this disease?"

The king said whining in pain, "You are an inexperienced doctor; you have just finished your course. You are a novice in this field. How will the history of the disease serve your purpose? Just tell me what medicines you propose to prescribe for me."

Bodhisatva said, "Maharaj! case-history of a patient is very important in order to have a correct diagnosis and administer correct medicines. A disease becomes easily curable when a doctor goes into the root cause of a problem and hits the very root of it."

The king explained to the doctor the shock that he had sustained by letting go the chance of bringing under his rule the three most opulent and prospering provinces. He said, "Doctor! This has been so shocking an incident to me that I have been cursing myself day and night. This incident has eaten away my health and vitality. Even at this hour I am worried about the loss sustained by me. This is something I cannot explain."

Bodhisatva delved deeply into the root of the disease and diagnosed his problem. The king, perhaps, wouldn't have been satisfied, had he suggested some remedy to him straightaway. So after giving a prolonged thought, he asked, "Maharaj! Will it be possible for you to bring those three provinces under your rule, if you continue to worry like this?"

"No, doctor! Now it is beyond my reach. What is gone is gone," said the king in a sad tone. Then taking a long breath he said, "It was all my mistake. I was so overpowered by greed and selfishness that I did not remember to extend due hospitality to him; nor did I care to enquire about the location of those provinces. I immediately began planning to launch an attack on those provinces. Oh, it was all my mistake."

Bodhisatva said, "So, what worries you now? Why do you bother? Your kingdom is no less opulent and prospering. There is no shortage of anything. Enjoy what you have. Do not have lust for more than what you require. One bed is sufficient for one person; he doesn't sleep in four beds at a time. Then why worry for four when you already have one? What you already have is more than sufficient for you. What will you do with those provinces. They will be in excess of requirement for you. And wasting one's valuable life on useless things is foolish. Please say no to lust and be content. There is no end to lust, greed, and desire; the more you get, the more you desire. So, don't bring unnecessary complications to your life. Remember—There is no substitute to contentment."

This had a positive effect on the king. He was feeling light now. He said, "All right! Now please suggest to me some medicine for my stomach problem."

Bodhisatva said, "Basically it is not stomach problem; it is in fact mental problem. That's precisely the reason why I went into the depth of the problem, and my discourse was aimed at opening your eyes. I am sure you will benefit from my discourse and regain your health."

The king realised his folly and agreed to get rid of lust and greed. He had also realised that crying for something that had already happened was nothing but sheer foolishness. And really, the king regained his health without being administered any medicine.

Someone has correctly said—there is no end to desires. Fulfilment of one desire gives rise to another desire; and thus people waste their valuable lives in fulfilling their desires only, and at the end, they end up having achieved nothing in particular. We must learn to exercise restraint and have self-control in order to be able to lead a happy and peaceful life.

❑ ❑

14

THE VANITY OF THE JACKAL

A hungry jackal was wandering in a forest. Hunger is something that is capable of driving even the greatest ones mad; and this exactly was the sitaution, the jackal was in. Hungry and exhausted he was moving around in the jungle, when suddenly a lion came before him. The jackals are supposed to be the cleverest and the most cunning of all animals. They are very quick in taking advantage of a situation. This jackal also did the same. As soon as he saw a lion standing before him, he spoke in a very humble manner, "I offer thousands of salutations to the king of the forest."

"Hello brother! How are you?"

"Maharaj! Your subjects in your kingdom are always very happy and comfortable. Yes, sometimes a small creature like me has to face certain problems."

"And what are your problems, Jackal?"

"Maharaj! First of all I am a Jackal; secondly I am alone, and thirdly I am starving. Now you yourself tell me, how shall I be happy. I am destined to be distressed. I can't even dream of happiness."

"You seem to be in a state of great distress."

"Yes, master! I can bear no more the burden of misfortunes. Sometimes I feel that it is better to die than leading such a sad life," said the jackal with tears welled up in his eyes.

"You have had enough of it, my friend. Don't weep! If you are so sad, please come with me and stay in my den in my company. Now you need not worry about your food or anything."

The jackal became very happy in his heart and accompanied him. Both reached the den after some time. The jackal's hunger increased manyfolds to see flesh lying in abundance in the den.

"Friend! You must be terribly hungry! Isn't it?"

"Yes Maharaj! Only I know how hungry I am."

"Then eat as much as you can. See, there is elephant's flesh lying in the corner. Eat to your heart's content. It is so much in quantity that you can assuage your hunger many times."

"Thank you, Maharaj! Thank you very much!"

Saying this the jackal fell upon the flesh and began eating it with delight.

He had been starving for the last so many days.

But today as if God had become very kind to him and it was sheer providence that he had met the lion. And the rest he managed using his wits. Now his future was secured; especially food was no problem to him anymore.

Having assuaged himself fully, the jackal fell asleep and began snoring lying there.

Next day in the morning when the lion set out in search of prey, he too was ready to accompany him.

He knew that the lion would hunt for himself, and so he would be able to appease his hunger by eating the leftover pieces of flesh.

And then, being in the company of the king of the forest would elevate his position also.

But the lion said, "Friend! You stay in the den and relax. You are my guest. I am going in search of prey. I shall bring something for you also to eat."

"Maharaj! You are the king of this forest. Going alone doesn't suit your status. A king should always be accompanied by his minister."

"Yes, what you say is logical. A king should not move alone. It is against the prestige of a king. He must be accompanied by a minister at least. All right! I appoint you my minister from today."

And the lion appointed the jackal his minister with immediate effect.

After becoming minister he was no more the same jackal. His was a position that was next to the lion in the forest. He began enjoying an elevated status. He was respected by big and small animals alike. But for the very small animals he had become a terror.

One day the lion called him and said, "Minister! From tomorrow you will have to guard the hill facing us, and it will be your duty to keep me informed of any enemy coming this side."

"But, Maharaj! What will be the mode of communication? Tell me some code."

"All that you have to do is to start howling when you see an enemy. I shall come and kill him. First, I shall fill my stomach with the prey, and with the left-over you will manage."

"As you wish, Maharaj! I am leaving right now."

The jackal went to that hill and began looking around vigilantly.

The jacal saw an elephant coming, after some time.

He immediately informed the lion of it and said, "Maharaj! A blood-thirsty elephant has entered your zone and his intentions don't seem to be good."

Hearing this the lion became very angry. He gave a mighty roar. His eyes began glowing like embers. His loud roaring caused the small animals of the forest to run for cover in order to save their lives.

The lion rushed to the hill.

He became very excited to see the elephant and pounced upon him with all his energy.

The elephant was also no less brave. He trumpeted so loud that the whole forest was shaken.

And then a fierce battle ensued between them.

Their fight was creating such loud noise as if two big mountains had collided with each other. But the drawback with the elephant was that he didn't have claws like lions; and the lion was clever enough to cling to a ruse and launch an attack on the hind portion of the elephant. The elephant was unable to reach his trunk behind in self-defence; and the lion taking advantage of the situation tore a chunk of flesh from his waist, thus rendering him weak on his hind legs. Ultimately the lion succeeded in killing the elephant. He began eating the flesh of the elephant with great delight.

It was after a very long time that he had got elephant's flesh to eat.

The lion was tearing the hide of the elephant with his sharp claws and pointed teeth, and eating the delicious flesh; and the jackal was watching him eating his kill with greedy eyes.

He was waiting for the lion to permit him to come and eat the flesh. He was cursing the lion in his heart—'I don't know how long this wretched fellow will continue to eat. Once he leaves the place, I too shall get a chance to assuage my hunger.'

After some time the lion, fully satiated, cleaning his whiskers with his tongue, said, "Minister! I am off now; please appease your hunger also."

"Maharaj! You have hardly eaten anything. Please have a little more."

"No, no! I have already eaten to my heart's content; no more please," saying this the lion went away.

The jackal fell upon the half-eaten elephant as soon as the lion turned back.

He was eating gluttonously, tearing out big pieces and swallowing them. Soon he had eaten his fill.

He looked at the sky and said, "O the Almighty! I am extremely thankful to you, for it is Thee who helped me make friends with the lion—it definitely is the result of my good deeds."

In a few days the jackal had changed completely.

Fooding and lodging is the basic need of everyone; and one, free from these worries, ought to become carefree and happy. The same was the situation, the jackal was in. Living with the lion had rendered him free from all worries; and he was getting fat and fatter day by day. Within a very short time he became so fat that the animals in the forest would get frightened to see him.

This inflated his ego so much that he began considering it unnecessary to have any support of the lion.

"Why should I now eat the ort of the lion?" One day he thought like this, "Now I have become so strong that I can even kill an elephant."

The jackal went to the lion, wished him and said, "O the king of the forest! I have served you for quite a long duration; I have come to take leave of you; in fact, I wish to go home."

"Friend! I have no objection to your leaving this place; but remember one thing—always keep in reserve for tomorrow from whatever you get to eat today. So long as you were with me you didn't have to worry about your food, but..."

"Maharaj! I have learnt the ways of hunting in your company; now I am strong enough to kill my prey and assuage my hunger."

The lion looked at the jackal attentively—today this jackal is looking very fat and lively; and the day he met me for the first time, he was merely a structure of bones. Eating without having to do anything for it, has made him so fat that he looks like an elephant calf now. Perhaps this is the reason why he considers himself brave now.

He thinks being fat means being strong. This kind of misconception will lead him to hell.

Still the lion was being sympathetic towards him. In order to show the real aspects of life, he said—

"Look dear jackal! I am aware that a little relief from problems can throw anyone off balance—you too have enjoyed every comfort in my company—and now you have begun considering yourself as brave and strong as I; but remember one thing—everyone is not capable of hunting; my sincere advice is that you stay with me till the end of your life and enjoy every comfort in my company. I am aware of the fact that you neither have a home nor you have to go anywhere. It is only the ego of your so called power and strength that is rising its head; and this is something extremely bad and unfortunate. Never forget that vanity brings only doom."

"O the king of the forest! You are absolutely correct; but now I wish to have an opportunity to live on my own. For once please let me be independent. You are my king, and have been my mentor as well; I only need your blessings to be successful in my life."

"If you consider yourself capable of hunting Jackal Maharaj, you take my place as a king from today, and I as your minister, will go in search of prey for you, that is I shall start performing your duties from today, and you shall take care of my kingdom. My job would be to look for a prey for you and as soon as I locate one, I shall come and inform you of it."

This was something beyond dreams for the jackal. There was a beam of satisfaction in his eyes. He was simply overwhelmed with joy. But outwardly he showed a little of hesitation and said, "All right, Maharaj! if this is what you wish. At least this will enable me to prove my strength and capability."

"All right! Now I am off in search of a prey for you. I am going towards the hill."

Saying this the lion set out towards the hill, and the jackal, as soon as the lion turned his back, sat on the throne of the lion, as if he had been waiting for it. This was the happiest moment of his life. He was feeling like bursting into laughter; he wanted to tell the whole world at the top of his voice that he had become a king; a king who can do anything and everything.

The delight of becoming a king had turned him blind. He had remained utterly quashed throughout his life. But today the position was different. Today a lion was his minister, his servant, and he was his master. This kind of realisation had driven him mad. He began looking madly at the throne of the lion, and then he began looking around with pride.

The small animals of the forest knew that the jackal was lion's friend. They always paid respect to him. But the jackal had failed to realise that those small animals offered their salutes to him only because he was the friend of the lion. And he always thought that they respected him for his own might.

Vanity is the enemy of everyone. It only leads to hell.

On the other side, the lion, sitting on the hill, was watching the animals come and go. For the first time in his life he was feeling completely relaxed. He didn't have to hunt today. Today the job of hunting had to be carried out by the jackal—the new king.

Just then the lion saw an elephant coming towards the forest. Instinctively he ran towards the elephant to make an attack. But he suddenly remembered that he had changed places with the jackal, and now it was the jackal who was supposed to hunt in his place. The lion came running to the jackal and said, "Maharaj! Please get into action. Your prey—an elephant—has come."

"What did you say? A prey has come? O dear! I am a king and hunting is a kind of sport for us. Come on, my minister! Let's go."

Saying this the jackal began roaring like a lion. The lion simpered to see him trying to roar like him.

"Why minister! Isn't my roaring frightening?"

"Yes, Maharaj! There is so much power in your roar that the small animals of this forest must have run away by now to save their lives."

"Such is the quality of a king! Don't I look exactly like an elephant?"

"Yes, yes, Maharaj! You look exactly like an elephant. But now please hurry up, or else that elephant..."

"Come on, minister! Follow me! I shall reach there before you and kill the elephant."

The jackal was fully confident that it wouldn't take him time to kill the elephant. After all he had seen the lion killing an elephant, and now he knew how to kill a prey like an elephant.

The elephant was trumpeting fiercely.

In a counter reply the jackal also began roaring. He reached in front of the elephant, took a long leap and pounced upon the elephant.

The lion also used to pounce in the same manner. He was following the footsteps of the lion.

When the elephant saw a jackal pouncing upon him, he became terribly angry. "How could a jackal attack him?" thought the elephant. He didn't wait another moment. He caught the jackal by his trunk, lifted him in the air and slammed him down.

The jackal was badly injured, and in a last bid to save his life, he tried to stand on his fours; but the elephant was so angry that he again caught him by his trunk and, this time, instead of lifting him in the air and again dashing him against the ground, he put his mighty feet on his stomach and made him sleep for ever.

The lion was standing at a distance and laughing. He only said— 'This fool has died an untimely death.'

❏ ❏

15

PUNISHED FOR SELFISHNESS

The cycle of births and rebirths has been given a great recognition in Buddhism. A creature dies and is reborn, and then again it dies, and thus this birth and rebirth system continues in a cyclic order. Based on this theory is a story of Bodhisatva, who during the reign of king Brahmadatta, took birth in the form of an elephant in the forests of Himachal.

This elephant calf was white like milk. And a calf of this kind had never been born in the family of elephants before.

Time kept rolling on and the calf continued growing. His capacity of understanding things grew with his age. His friends followed instincts and they did many things that he never liked. For example—his friends, in their playfulness, would shake the branches of trees and make the nests of birds fall; trample the small and innocent creatures under their feet and kill them; or hold them in their trunks and toss them in the air.

One day he became very restless and decided to isolate himself. He had developed a great affinity with the other animals of the forest.

He never bothered any animal, and lived with them with considerable understanding. His behaviour was such that all the animals were very happy with him, but at the same time they were also very much surprised. They had never seen an elephant who cared so much for small animals.

One day that white elephant was going in the forest. He saw a monkey sitting on a branch of a tree and weeping. He looked very weak.

"O brother! Why are you sitting alone and weeping?"

"Brother! I am weeping because the other monkeys, finding me of weak constitution, trouble me very much. What else can I do except weeping?"

"This is very sad. These monkeys make fun of their own brother who is weak; they bother him. This is something they should never do. You please come with me; I shall talk to them. This is highly improper for anyone to torture and oppress someone who is weak."

Saying this, the elephant made him sit on his back and took him to his friends. Apart from the monkeys, the other animals of the forest were also surprised to see a lean and thin monkey sitting on the back of the elephant.

The elephant was welcomed when he reached the dwelling place of monkeys.

"Hello! King of elephants! What made you take the trouble of coming to the dwelling place of the poors?" asked the chief of monkeys after welcoming him.

"Brothers! I have come to intercede with you all for this freind of mine. I have come to make a request, and I hope you will not turn down my request."

"You need not make requests to us. Maharaj! You are our saviour; you are king of elephants. By making requests to us you would be putting us to shame. On the contrary we are here to obey your orders."

"Look, brothers! The monkey you are seeing on my back, belongs to your community; he is your brother. Why do you hate one of your brothers who is weak? Just because he is weaker than you? It's a matter of shame for all of you."

Al the monkeys became silent to hear the elephant. What could they say, after all?"

"Why don't you think that every creature is weaker than some other creature? This is nature's arrangement. It all depends on the will of God. He has made some creatures very strong, and at the same time you will find that some creatures are weak in constitution and delicate; but this does not mean that the strong ones should torture and oppress the poor ones. Never forget that there are very strong ones also existing on the earth."

All the monkeys were ashamed of their behaviour. There was

absolute silence for some time, and then suddenly the chief of the monkeys said, "What you say is correct, O the king of elephants! These monkeys will definitely be punished for their ill behaviour towards your friend."

"Look, brother! I don't intend to punish them. My intention is to create an understanding among you. I shall tell you a story and this will throw some light on the characteristics of creatures."

"All right! O king of elephants! Please tell us the story."

The elephant became silent for some time. He made the monkey alight from his back and asked him to sit with the other monkeys. All the monkeys were silently watching the white elephant, who was going to tell them a story.

The elephant, addressing them all, began his story—"Brothers! once a traveller was going through a jungle all alone. The forest was so dense that it was hardly possible to see anything. This resulted into disorientation. Now he was extremely worried. He began trembling with fear. He saw an elephant coming towards him in the dim light of the forest. This frightened him so much that he lost his nerves. 'O God! What should I do now. It wouldn't take time for the fierce elephant to kill me. O God! Please save me from this trouble'—muttering these words he ran in the opposite direction to save his life. In the process of running in a confused manner, he continued praying to God for safety of his life. He was panting and his face had become red. When his legs could take him no more and he began staggering, he stopped and looked back with a hope that he must have left the elephant behind and was out of danger. But the scene was on the contrary. The elephant was standing at a short distance from him. He looked timidly at him, his heart in his mouth.

The elephant said, "Brother! You are a stranger in this forest. I came to enquire about your well-being when I saw you worried and sad; I wanted to know if I could be of some use to you. But you are unnecessarily frightened of me and running away. Brother! it's not wise to be afraid of someone for no apparent reason."

Now the traveller was looking at the elephant wide-eyed. He couldn't believe his ears; he was not able to make out whether he was hearing an elephant or it was a voice from the space.

"Tell me, brother! What's the matter? Why are you so worried?"

"Brother! O king of elephants! I was going to VAranasi; but I got disorientated in this forest, and this is the reason why I am so worried and troubled."

"You need not worry, my friend! You please come along with me to my house and halt there. You will have no problem there. Relax and organise yourself and then I shall guide you out of this forest."

The elephant took him to his care, made him comfortable, and went out to bring some fruits for him.

Eating fresh and tasty fruits relieved the traveller of his tiredness. He slept in the cave peacefully. The elephant had already made arrangements for his breakfast before he woke up in the morning. The traveller was surprised to see all this. This was for the first time that he was seeing this kind of animal.

"Friend! Please finish your breakfast, and then I shall carry you on my back to Varanasi."

"O king of elephants! You are indeed very kind. Till now I had been under the impression that elephants are of murderous tendency—they kill human beings."

"All creatures are not alike, friend! Good and bad, all kinds of creatures are there in this world. Neither all are good nor all are bad."

"You are no ordinary creature, O king of elephants; you are a god."

"I am at everyone's service; I wish everyone good. From today you are my friend. You may come to me any time you are in need of my help. I shall help you in every possible way."

"I thank you very much for the kind offer."

After that the elephant made the traveller sit on his back, took him to Varanasi and returned. The traveller registered in his memory the route through which the elephant took him to Varanasi. After many days, the traveller whose name was Garibdas went out to see the market. He saw a shop in which there were many very beautiful things made of ivory.

He went into the shop and began talking to the craftsman who had made carved ornaments of ivory—"You have made very beautiful things."

"Brother! I can make even more beautiful things. But what to do? Here the position is that even after paying handsomely, it is not possible to get good quality elephant tusks."

"Do you carve these ornaments out of live elephant's tusks?"

"Brother! one can't even dream of live elephant's tusks. Who has the guts to extract the tusks of a live elephant?"

"Will you buy it if someone brings a live elephant's tusk for you?"

"I am prepared to pay to his demand, but who can bring it?

The craftsman looked in disbelief at Garibdas and became busy with his work.

"Look, brother! There isn't anything impossible in the world. It's not that I am boasting; but let me tell you that I can bring the tusks of a live elephant."

"All right, brother! If you manage to do it, I shall not only congratulate you, I shall also pay you handsomely."

The craftsman was confident that Garibdas would be able to bring neither live nor dead elephant's tusks.

Such people keep dreaming of becoming rich and die in a poor state of life.

"Look at this fool! His name is Garibdas* and he wants to deal in ivory business," the craftsman thought to himself.

Garibdas had the wild elephant in his mind, who had become his friend; and who had brought him on his back upto Varanasi. He was confident that the elephant would help him. Once again Garibdas went to the same forest; and it didn't take him time to locate the elephant. The elephant also understood that he must have come with some motive, because he had returned too soon.

---

* slave of the poors.

"Please accept my salutes, O king of elephants!" said Garibdas with folded hands.

"Hello! How is it that you have returned so soon?"

"Sir, you already know, my name is Garibdas."

"Yes, yes, I know it."

"That's what I want to tell you. Not only my name is Garibdas; I am poor in every respect. Now under these circumstances, it has become impossible for me to survive even."

"Now what is it that you want from me, Garibdas?"

"Just give me one of your tusks, so that I may sell it and do some business. This will enable me to earn bread and butter for my wife and children."

"If your circumstances are such, I am prepared to give both my tusks. But you shall have to cut them."

"I have brought a saw with me for this purpose. Just help me get rid of poverty. May you live long."

The kind elephant sat on the ground. Garibdas sawed both his tusks. He was very happy thinking that the days of his poverty had come to an end. Now he too would become rich. He will be considered among one of the rich ones.

"All right, friend! I thank you once again."

"Look, friend! Never forget one thing—my these two tusks are a source of widsom and conscience; I have given away the most essential part of my life to you. And this I have done because you are my friend."

"Yes, yes, brother! I know you are very kind. It's impossible to get a true friend like you in this world."

Saying this Garibdas took leave of him and left.

From the forest he went straight to the shop of the craftsman; the person with whom he had had a deal.

"Brother! Take this; a live elephant's tusks," saying this he put the tusks before him.

The craftsman looked at the tusks carefully, and then he looked at the untidy clothes of Garibdas. He was not able to understand how he could manage a live elephant's tusks. His experienced eyes had assessed the genuineness of the tusks. When Garibdas saw the craftsman silent, he asked, "Why sir, what's the problem? Are they not real?"

"No, no, they are real," said the craftsman still looking at Garibdas in utter disbelief.

"Then make payment and allow me to leave. I have brought these tusks for you with great difficulty. Now please don't delay; make the payment."

The craftsman gave him fifty gold coins. Garibdas began trembling to see fifty gold coins. His happiness knew no bounds. He couldn't believe all this; he thought he was dreaming. It took him some time to believe what he was seeing. He said to himself—'Now I am no more a poor man; I am a rich man now.'

Now he was worried about the safety of those fifty gold coins.

Someone has correctly said—'a poor man loses his balance to see a lot of money at a time before him.' This exactly was the situation

Garibdas was in.

On the one hand Garibdas was very happy and on the other he was worried about the safety of the gold coins. Somehow he managed to reach his house and said to his wife in a trembling voice, "Darling! We have become rich now. Look, we have become rich. See! only rich people have these coins; and today we also have these coins. Come on! We shall go to market and eat whatever we like. We shall also make heavy purchases today."

Garibdas took his wife to market.

There was a time when Garibdas could not afford to buy sweets; he would look at the sweet shops and take a heavy breath—thinking that they were beyond his reach. But today he was not the same Garibdas. He went to those shops with his wife, and they ate to their hearts' content. After having eaten their fill, they bought good clothes for everyone in their family. They also bought items of decoration for their house.

The world of Garibdas had changed.

Next day—

He went to see his old friends, riding on a horse. Everyone of his acquaintance in the town was surprised to see him. They were wondering how he had become so rich suddenly. He had become the talk of the town.

"Where did this mad fellow get so much money from?"

"He seems to have got some buried treasure from somewhere."

Becoming rich overnight is a miracle; so everyone had one's own guess about the source of his wealth.

Garibdas invited his friends to his house and offered them dishes according to their tastes. Days of lavish living pass very quickly. Getting wealth suddenly and that too without having to work hard for it, leads one to aimless merry-making. This is a period of life when even enemies become friends. And similarly, in the absence of money, even friends become enemies.

Garibdas was spending lavishly and open heartedly on his friends;

and the number of his friends was growing day by day.

Sitting idle and spending mercilessly brings an end to any amount of money. The same thing happened to Garibdas also. Very soon he had squandered all his money. Now once again he was a poor man. He could not survive without money. What bothered him most was—how would he face his friends?

Once again he was reminded of his poverty, and then his chain of thoughts reminded him of his benefactor—the elephant. He remembered that he had cut and brought only the halves of the elephant's tusks. And as soon as he remembered this, his eyes beamed with joy and hope. He thought—'I had cut only the halves of the elephant's tusks. Why not go and ask for the remaining halves also.'

Thinking this he set out to the forest on the next day.

The elephant had seen his friend coming from quite a distance. He welcomed Garibdas when he reached near him. He said, "Hello friend! How are you?"

"Brother! I have come to you once again."

"It's my pleasure, brother! You may come here everyday if you want. What's the matter, anyway? Are you having some problem?"

"Brother! I don't know how to broach the topic. But still, ...I have no alternative; I have to tell you. In fact, I managed to clear all my debts with the money I got by selling your tusks. Now I want to start a new business, and I have no money for it. I am in need of some money."

"Garibdas! You need not worry. Even if you can be happy at the cost of my life, I am ready to do it. You are a friend of mine; and there is a saying—a friend in need is a friend indeed."

"I have hit the target," thought Garibdas, and without waiting another moment he began cutting the remaining halves of his tusks with his saw.

The elephant was sacrificing his splendour and beauty in the name of friendship; he was giving away his tusks, whereas his friend was spoiling his life for his pleasure, for merry-making.

He did not even care to think about the life of the poor animal whose tusks he was cutting for his selfish ends. Selfish Garibdas deprived the animal of his splendour for his own happiness.

The elephant had sacrificed everything in the name of friendship, and Garibdas...? He was dancing with happiness thinking that he would become very rich by selling away the tusks.

He was thinking that he would be living in a palatial building like rich people; he would employ servants. He would change his name from Garibdas to Amirdas.

What do I care for that silly animal? After all, he has to live in the forest only. Now there are no tusks left with him. I can break the ties of friendship with him now. What's the use of having friendship with someone who doesn't have anything valuable?

He had every prospects of becoming rich now.

He was running in great speed through the forest. And suddenly, in a place where he put his feet, the ground cracked and there was a deep fissure. The feet of Garibdas were firmly caught in the fissure and it became impossible for him to free himself.

And then there was fire in the fissure, sending thousands of pointed steams of flames as if ready to devour him. His feet were fixed firmly in the deep crack; he was trying to free himself—crying in pain. But nature had its own decision. The fire, which rose from nowhere, was lolling its tongues, licking him from head to feet and devouring him gradually. After some time there were no shrieks of pain and Garibdas had completely disappeared in the brilliance of yellow flames. Now neither there was a trace of Garibdas nor of the tusks; both had been swallowed by the hungry flames. Slowly the fire died down. Suddenly there was a grave voice from the heavens—'A sinner, a greedy, and a selfish man can never be satisfied; even if he is given the whole world in his possession, he will not be at peace. He would still be wanting more.'

And thus, that selfish and greedy man got what he rightly deserved.

❑ ❑

16

MISERLY TREASURER

KOSHIA was a treasurer in the court of the Sultan. He used to perform his duties honestly and sincerely. Everyone was very happy with him. He was very kind to the poor. He was dead honest and very loyal to the Sultan. On the whole Koshia was a person who embraced all the superlatives. He had only one drawback; he was miserly beyond measure.

One evening when Koshia returned home, he was very sad. He didn't say anything to his wife; he simply went and lay in his bed.

"What's wrong with you? Are you all right?" asked his wife to see him lying disconsolately in his bed.

"Oh, yes! I am all right."

"Then why is it that you are lying in your bed and looking so dejected? Have you had a quarrel with someone in the court?"

"No, no, not at all!"

"Then what is it that bothers you?"

"Darling! Why do you want to know? It's no use. Please leave me alone."

"Darling! How is it possible? I can bear any amount of pain, but I cannot see you lying sunk in melancholy. Is there any wife who can bear to see her husband in a state of dejection?

"Radha! My darling! Now how to tell you? While I was on my way to home, I saw people eating Pooris* at a sweetmeat shop, and enjoying it thoroughly."

"You should have also eaten."

"How could I?"

"Why? What was the problem?"

* unleavened cake fried in clarified butter.

"Wouldn't I have to pay for it?"

"You are treasurer of the Sultan; not an ordinary man. You have got sufficient money to spend on yourself; you can eat whatever you like."

"But how can I spend so much at a time? Being treasurer of the Sultan does not mean that I should keep squandering my money."

"If that is so, I shall myself cook Pooris for you at home. And you will see how delicious it will be."

"Radha! Can you cook Pooris for me?"

"Yes, of course! Why not? I shall cook Pooris for you and send some to our neighbours also. I am sure they will become very happy to get Pooris from us."

"No, no, Radha! You will be causing me a heavy loss that way. Pooris are not for distribution."

"All right! I shall not give Pooris to our neighbours. I shall cook just enough Pooris sufficient for our children, for you and me."

"No, no! Even that would be a bit too expensive. You already know, giving children too much to eat, spoils them. It spoils their digestive system also."

Koshia's wife knew only too well about her husband. She knew why people call him an extremely miserly person."

"What are you thinking darling?" asked Koshia seeing his wife lost in thoughts.

"No, no, nothing! I was just thinking that I shall cook tasty Pooris and then both of us will enjoy eating them, together."

"But, darling!" He was going to say something, but suddenly checked himself.

"Yes, yes! What is it? You were going to say something."

"In fact, I am thinking......"

"Please don't hesitate! Tell me! What are you thinking?"

"What I wanted to say is that it is I who wants to eat Pooris..."

"Yes?"

"Then why should you eat? No, No! Please don't misunderstand. What I mean to say is—if I have an intense desire to eat something, it is only I who should eat. Why should you also eat? You know this kind of unnecessary expenditure causes avoidable loss."

Radha was quick to understand what her husband had meant. She knew everything but didn't say anything. She simply laughed and said, "Doesn't matter! I shall cook Pooris for you only. Is that all right?"

"That's all right! But if you cook Pooris in the kitchen, our neighbours will get the nice smell of it and come asking for Pooris."

"Then...?" Radha was in a fix.

"I personally feel that you take everything to the roof and start cooking Pooris in the open air. No one will be able to see us there. And then you will go on cooking and serving hot Pooris to me."

Radha listened to him patiently, but she was feeling a little unhappy now. Taking everything to the roof and then bringing them down—it will be unnecessary labour and will take a lot of time also. "O God! This is too much," she thought to herself. But then she thought she had to do all that if she was a caring wife. She had to do all that for the sake of her husband. After all a husband is God. If God is pleased, the whole world is pleased.

Thinking this Radha began carrying all the cooking material to the roof.

Within a short time she had taken all the necessary things to the roof. Her husband was sitting on a cot by her side, and she was cooking Pooris.

It took her hardly any time to cook Pooris for her husband; and her husband—Koshia—was feeling very happy to see hot Pooris before him. For how long he had been thinking of eating Pooris, but fear of expenditure had always compelled him to suppress his desire. But today he, somehow, had managed to gather enough courage to get Pooris cooked for himself.

"Aha! What nice smell!" said he. He got down from his cot and sat cross-legged by the side of his wife. Just as his wife had served Pooris to him, he saw a Buddhist monk coming towards their house.

"Darling! Our trouble starts now."

"What has happened, my master? Why are you so worried?"

"Look there! A Buddhist monk is coming. These beggars are too much."

"Making charities doesn't make someone poor! Like taking out water from a river doesn't make it shallow."

"Your philosophy doesn't bear any logic. Money is earned, whereas water comes from mountains. Look! I am not going to give him anything. I have got these Pooris cooked for myself; not for this beggar."

The Buddhist monk kept watching them silently, without speaking a word.

"Is he dumb?" asked Koshia, seeing the monk silent.

"No, he is not dumb. He is a Buddhist monk. He won't speak. He himself will go away, if you give him something."

"All right! You do one thing; cook a small Poori for him and give him. Hurry up! Or else, seeing him here other beggars will also start collecting here."

"As you wish," saying this she took a very small dough of flour and began rolling it to make a Poori. But miraculously this Poori outsized the other Pooris that she had cooked for her husband. Radha was simply flabbergasted to see this miracle.

"Better you take this one; I shall cook another one for the monk." Radha gave that Poori to her husband.

This time she took an even smaller dough of flour. The Buddhist monk was standing patiently, maintaining absolute silence.

Radha couldn't believe her eyes. She was looking at the Poori wide-eyed. This time the Poori had become even bigger.

"What is all this? No matter how small dough of floor I roll, the size of Poori is going on increasing. I fail to understand anything." Radha was totally confused. She looked at the Buddhist monk who was still standing speechless. Perhaps he was waiting for his share of Poori.

"What is this Radha? You have rolled an even bigger one this time. I had told you to give him a small Poori and ask him to leave. It's not proper to encourage beggars like this."

"What can I do, darling? I am trying my level best to roll as small a Poori as possible; but somehow it is getting larger by itself."

"All right!" You keep this Poori also; and cook a small Poori for him. Be careful this time and see that you don't cook a big one.

"All right!" Radha took yet another small dough of flour and began rolling it. She looked at the Buddhist monk who was still standing silently. He was so quiet that he seemed to be lost within.

"The same thing happened once again. This Poori outsized the earlier ones. Koshia looked at his wife angrily and said, "What the hell are you doing? I have been continuously telling you to cook a small Poori for the monk, and you are going on increasing the size everytime."

"What can I do? It's not within my control. It's all happening automatically."

"But I feel you aren't even trying to roll a small Poori. How is it possible that you are trying to roll small Pooris, and every time your Pooris are outsizing the earlier ones?" This time Koshia had become very angry.

"You can see for yourself that everytime I am taking a yet smaller dough of flour to roll a small Poori for the monk, and every time it becomes larger automatically. I am getting to feel now that I am under some kind of magic spell. And this I say because it had never happened before."

"All right! Give him one Poori so that he goes away from here. At least then I shall be able to sit peacefully and enjoy eating Pooris... What a problem? It is only because of this that I came to the roof, but this monk did not spare me even here."

"You need not worry. I shall give him a Poori and ask him to go away from here. And then you can sit and eat comfortably," saying this Radha tried to pick up one Poori; but again...another miracle. All the Pooris had stuck to each other.

"Look, darling! You see for yourself. All these Pooris have become inseparable. It's not possible to take out one Poori from the lot," said Radha to her husband.

"Give them to me. I shall separate them. This Buddhist monk has become a real problem for me. I had the Pooris cooked for myself, thinking that I shall eat and enjoy the taste of delicious Pooris in isolation, but this problem seems to have appeared just to spoil the fun." Koshia, once again looked at the monk with anger and hatred.

But Koshia was doubly surprised to see that even he could not separate the Pooris from each other. They were firmly fixed to each other. He tried his level best but could not succeed.

"Darling! It seems what you said was correct. All this miracle is taking place because of this man only. Really this man has cast some spell on us. I shall not eat these Pooris now."

"Radha! I am aware you did all this for me only; but now I personally feel that I am not destined to enjoy eating them. Now all these Pooris should be given to this strange beggar. I shall eat some other day."

"As you wish! A person trying to restrict an almsgiver is considered the greatest sinner. So, I wouldn't say anything to you."

"All right, darling! I am giving all these Pooris in alms to him. He will come and sit in my place and eat them," saying this Koshia got up from his place and said to the beggar, "Maharaj! Please come here and sit comfortably, and eat these Pooris; now I realise that it was all your share." But this time there was no tinge of hatred in his voice; rather his voice was tinged with regret.

"No, brother! I cannot eat them."

"Why?"

"I am a Buddhist monk. I don't want anything for myself. We have renounced the world and forgotten ourselves. We have no attachment with anything in the world. We have nothing like personal desire."

"Then what is it that you want, Maharaj?"

"Brother! You are a greedy human being. Detach yourself from worldly things and learn to live peacefully. This is what Lord Buddha has taught us. You will be pleasantly surprised to learn that Lord Buddha has arrived with hundreds of his disciples in your city."

"What did you say? Koshia and his wife were terribly surprised to hear this. They were not able to believe their own ears. They were looking at the beggar wide-eyed.

Seeing them looking at him wide-eyed he said, "I mean it, brother. All this food is for our spiritual teacher and messenger of peace—Lord Buddha and his disciples. How can I eat it alone?"

"O God! we have made a grave mistake—we looked at this Buddhist monk with hatred in our eyes...he is a great saint; he had come with the message of Lord Buddha; O God! we have committed a great sin..."

Koshia began weeping bitterly with his head in his hands.

"Expiation brings an end to sufferings caused by sinful acts. Brother! Don't worry. Once you go in the shelter of Lord Buddha, you will forget the whole world."

"Yes, yes, Maharaj! We both shall go in the shelter of Lord Buddha, and only then we shall be able to atone for our sins. We are sinners. We failed to realise that the person who has come to our house, is a messenger of God. And how foolish and sinful it has been to exhibit our hatred towards the messenger of God?"

"You please come with us," said the Buddhist monk.

"Yes, yes! I shall carry the basket of Pooris on my head to Lord Buddha. In fact, I am the real sinner. I shall have to beg forgiveness. My wife is not at all to be blamed. She has only been obeying me." Saying this Koshia took the basket of Pooris on his head and began moving behind the monk with his wife's hand in his hand. Koshia was thinking in the way 'how has all this happened? If he loved anything in his life, it was money. He had never wanted anything other than money. But this charismatic monk has changed everything today.'

Walking thus, they reached a dense forest. There was, in front of him, Lord Buddha himself sitting on a rostrum with his eyes closed. He was in meditation. He had a string of beads in his hand; he looked like an apostle of peace and love.

Koshia fell in his feet. His voice was trembling with fear, as if he had committed a great sin unknowingly—"I beg your forgiveness, O God. I am a great sinner. I haven't done any good deed till today. I am a worshipper of wealth. I have never made any charity in the name of God. I have never given good food to my wife and children.

"Kohsia! Always remember one thing. Human beings have been making mistakes ever since they have come into existence. But they start repenting when they get a blow. Remember—realising one's mistakes makes one great."

"Should I believe that you have pardoned me, Lord?" Koshia asked happily.

"Realising one's follies enables a person to attain enlightenment, and this enlightenment makes a person great...Koshia! Rise! and spread the splendour of wisdom far and wide; like one of my monks has done and shown you a new path. He has brought you into light from darkness. Now please offer these Pooris to my disciples with your own hands. They haven't eaten anything for the last so many days."

Koshia stood up and looked at the basket of Pooris, and then cast an eye at the Buddhist monks sitting in front of him. He was extremely worried, as the number of monks outnumbered the Pooris in his basket.

"What are you thinking, Koshia?" asked Lord Buddha to see him in a perplexed situation.

"Maharaj! How is this possible? There are hundreds of devotees sitting here, and there are very few Pooris in my basket. Who will eat them and how many of your devotees will be able to assuage their hunger? No, Maharaj! I shall not be able to do this. I cannot afford to offer Pooris to some and leave the other ones starving."

"Do not lose heart, Koshia. Even God honours faith and devotion. Have faith in God and start distributing Pooris among them. Try to appease the hunger of as many of my disciples as possible, and leave everything to God."

Koshia was a little disheartened. He was not happy with this kind of situation. He was worried about the number of Pooris, which was hardly enough to assuage the hunger of only one of the so many devotees sitting in front of him. All of them were hungry and wanted to eat.

"Come on! start distributing, Koshia. What are you looking at? My blessings are with you. Don't be disheartened. Have faith in God. Those who have firm faith in God, are helped by Him." Lord Buddha raised his hand and blessed him. A strange kind of light emitted from his eyes.

Koshia felt some kind of vibration in his body which filled him with energy and faith. He felt as if the whole of his body was undergoing some kind of change. Hundreds of Buddhist monks had their gaze fixed at him. Koshia said to his wife in her ears, "This is an hour of test for us. start giving one Poori each to each of the disciples. We shall try to feed as many as possible, and shall beg forgiveness of those who do not get any, after our stock exhausts.

"All right! We have to obey the orders of Lord Buddha," Radha remembered God with full faith and began distributing Pooris.

"O God! What kind of miracle is this! You are going on distributing Pooris and still the number of Pooris in the basket is just as many."

Gradually all the monks were served Pooris and they began eating them patiently. God knows for how many days they had been hungry.

Koshia and his wife were dumbfounded to see that all the monks had eaten their fill and still the number of Pooris in the basket had not decreased.

"This is all due to the blessings of Lord Buddha. You had never offered meals to anyone in your life. But today he has made you do it with your own hands. And at the same time he has saved your Pooris also," said Radha looking into the eyes of her husband.

Koshia understood that this was all God's play. He had been wandering in darkness till that day. This was the day of his enlightenment. Both, husband and wife, bowed before Lord Buddha— "You are great, O Lord! Our life has become meaningful with your kind blessings. We were sinners. You have enlightened us. ....I shall never do a sinful act in my life again. Now I take a vow that I shall never eat alone; I shall share with others, whatever I have." Koshia was standing before Lord Buddha with folded hands in benediction.

"Go, Koshia! Go; spread the splendour of wisdom throughout the world. This is the greatest worship."

Blessed by Lord Buddha, both—husband and wife—were returning home. Their faces glowed with the satisfaction of attainment of peace.

❑ ❑

17

BAD DEEDS BAD END

THERE lived a weaver in a village. He had two wives. He had one daughter each from both of them. Elder wife's daughter's name was Sukkhu and the younger wife's daughter's name was Dukkhu. According to her name, Sukkhu lived with her mother happily, because the weaver loved his elder wife and her daughter very much. Whereas Dukkhu and her mother were in an extreme state of distress, because the weaver never cared for them. Both, mother and daughter were humble and kind. They would remain busy in the household work from dawn to dusk, but would never complain about it.

One day the weaver died due to heart failure. After his death, Sukkhu's mother misappropriated all the property with great ingenuity and kicked them out of the house. Now Dukkhu and her mother would weave cloth whole day and somehow manage their bread and butter with the money they would get by selling it. On the contrary Sukkhu and her mother were passing their days happily and spending lavishly. Even then Sukkhu's mother was not satisfied. Day and night she used to keep planning to do some harm to Dukkhu's mother.

But she had not yet had an opportunity to do so. So many times she made plans, tried to execute them, but every time, by sheer providence, Dukkhu's mother escaped her ill designs.

One day Dukkhu's mother left some cotton outside in the sun for drying, and telling her daughter to keep a watch, she herself went to a nearby pond to fetch some water. Suddenly wind began blowing in sharp gusts, and before Dukkhu could understand anything or do anything, it took away all the cotton with itself. Dukkhu tried to collect the cotton but in vain. At last she gave up and began weeping bitterly. The god of wind saw her weeping and felt pity on her.

He materialized before her and began consoling her. He said, "Dukkhu! you follow me; I shall have your cotton retrieved."

Dejected Dukkhu met a cow in the way. The cow requested her to clean the cow dung around her, and feed her green grass. Dukkhu did it and left the place.

She had gone only a few steps when a banana tree stopped her and requested her to clean the dirt around. Having cleaned the dirt she had hardly gone a few steps when a horse stopped her, and requested her to get him some grass and water.

Having satisfied everyone, she moved forward. She saw an old lady with white hair, deeply engrossed in spinning yarn. And miraculously the spinned yarn was automatically getting converted into beautiful sarees.

The god of wind told Dukkhu that the old lady was Moon's mother. He also told her to ask the old lady for her cotton.

When Dukkhu touched the old mother's feet humbly and asked for her cotton, she blessed her and said, "My sweet daughter! First go, take a bath and eat something. There is a towel in the front room, there are some sarees in another room; you can take any saree you like. There is some hair oil in the third room; put it in your hair and take a dip in the pond which is behind my house. And then I shall return your cotton."

As ordered by the old mother, Dukkhu took a towel and went in the other room; she was simply dumbstruck to see so many expensive sarees there; but she chose the simplest one for herself, and the oil she selected to put in her hair, too, was of a very ordinary type. She set out to the pond.

Just as she had taken a dip in the pond, she was transformed into a beautiful fairy. But as there was no mirror around, she could not become aware of the development. She took one more dip and there was another miracle. Now she was heavily laden with expensive and beautiful ornaments. She was frightened to see this miracle, and could not dare take another dip. She came out of the pond and went straight to the old mother.

The old mother asked her to go to the dining room to have her meals. There were different kinds of dainty dishes arranged at the dining table. But Dukkhu was a different kind of girl. Despite being poor, she was not greedy. She took simple food and that too in a very little quantity, and assuaged her hunger. The old mother gently caressed her hair and said, "Go, my daughter! Go to the fourth room. There are many small boxes filled with cotton. You can take any box you like."

Dukkhu went to the fourth room and thinking that she was a poor girl and she should take a thing that suited her status, she took the smallest box and came back to the old mother. She took her blessings and set out to her home.

While she was on the way to her home, the horse gave her a pitcher full of gold coins, the banana tree gave her a compact pendent bunch of golden banana, and the cow gave her a young cow who could be milked any time. Now Dukkhu wanted to reach home with all those gifts at the earliest. She knew her mother must be getting worried to find her missing.

Dukkhu reached home after some time and called her mother. Dukkhu's mother came running as soon as she heard her voice,but she was stunned to see her completely transformed.

After hearing the whole sequence of happenings, Dukkhu's mother thanked God and said, "Oh, my darling! My sweet daughter! it's nothing but God's grace."

Dukkhu's mother went to Sukkhu's mother and very humbly, she offered to share the gifts. But Sukkhu's mother was filled with jealousy and refused to share the gifts straightaway.

Feeling greatly insulted, Dukkhu and her mother returned home. They opened the box of cotton in the night. But instead of cotton they saw a very handsome prince coming out of the box. They were simply overwhelmed to see him. The prince married Dukkhu and all the three began living happily.

Seeing this Sukkhu's jealous mother also planned to send her daughter to the old mother. She, in a bid to follow the exact sequence

of happenings, kept some cotton outside for drying. Suddenly gusts of wind took away her cotton also, and the god of wind asked Sukkhu to follow him.

Sukkhu began following him in great speed. The cow, the banana tree, and the horse tried to stop her in the way, asking for the same favours; but she gave them a disdainful look, and continued moving in the same speed.

She did not even care to wish when she saw the old mother, and asked her to give her also the box of cotton in gift. The old mother listened to her patiently, and asked her also to do things that she had asked Dukkhu to do. And Sukkhu in all her greediness, selected the costliest Saree for herself; then she put scented oil in her hair, and taking a big mirror, went to take dips in the pond. She closed her eyes and within moments she took three to four dips in the pond. But when she posed before the mirror to see her image, she was terribly frightened. She was horrified to see herself in such a form.

She looked ugly like an ogress. She screamed with fear and went running to the old mother. The old mother said, "This is all due to your greediness. You forgot my instructions and in a hurry you took two extra dips.

Then she asked Sukkhu to forget about it and directed her to go to the dining hall. There too, her greedy nature made her select the daintiest dishes for eating.

Having eaten gluttonously she belched in a very ugly manner and went straight to the room where boxes full of cotton were kept. She selected the biggest box and left the place without even saying good-bye to the old mother, and set out to her home muttering inaudibly.

In the way, the horse kicked her, the banana tree dropped a heavy bunch of bananas on her head, and the cow chased her with her pointed horns. Somehow, saving herself from all these, she managed to reach home. She was weeping bitterly. But the worse came to worst when her own mother refused to recognize her.

But when Sukkhu narrated her sad story, her dejected mother took it as her ill fate; she didn't say anything. Only one thing was left as hope, and that was the box filled with cotton. Her greedy mother suggested to her to open the box at night in isolation. When it became absolutely dark, she left Sukkhu alone in a room, bolted the door from outside and went to sleep.

Next day she kept waiting for her daughter, expecting her to come out of the room with a handsome prince. She unlatched the door from outside and began knocking at it. But when the door didn't open for a long time, she became very nervous. She took an axe and broke the door. The scene inside the room was ghastly.

What she saw was the skeleton of her daughter on one side, and a slough of a big python on the other. In a corner there was the box of cotton lying open.

Sukkhu's mother had been punished by nature for her bad deeds. Now she had no alternative except to weep and repent. That's why it is said that bad deeds have bad ends.

❏ ❏

18

TIT FOR TAT

There lived a camel in a village. Everyday he used to go to a nearby lush farm to graze. The camel was very simple and honest. There was a jackal who was his friend. But the jackal was very cunning and crafty. Often he used to ride the camel and at times he used to create problems also for him. But since the camel had never undergone any major problem due to his craftiness, he generally ignored his misdeeds.

One day the jackal said to him, "Brother camel! There is a big farm nearby; and I have seen big and tasty cucumbers in it. Let us go and eat them. For the last so many days I have been eating very ordinary and tasteless stuff, and I am tired of it. This will bring some change."

Cunning as he was, the jackal gave such a description of the cucumbers that the camel's mouth began watering with an immense desire to eat them, and he became so restless that he immediately set out to the farm. After reaching the farm the jackal began eating cucumbers; and since jackals are small in size, he had assuaged his hunger very soon. But the camel had hardly eaten anything. Meanwhile, since the jackal had already eaten his fill, he began howling loudly without caring for the camel. The camel tried to restrain the jackal from doing so, but the jackal wouldn't listen to him. He said, "What can I do, brother camel? I am helpless. Howling after eating something is a must for me. If I don't, I start feeling very uneasy," saying this, he began howling again,

Hearing a jackal howling, the owner of the farm came running to his farm with a big stick in his hand. The jackal saw him coming. Because of his small size, he managed to escape through bushes without being noticed. But poor camel, though he also tried to escape, was caught and beaten mercilessly.

This happening made the camel so angry that he stopped talking to the jackal.

The jackal also didn't come to see him for many days; but he had thoroughly enjoyed seeing the camel being beaten by the farm owner. As if this was not enough, he was looking for another such opportunity to get him thrashed again.

One day the jackal met the camel and said very humbly, "Brother camel! I am indeed very sorry for the happening on that day, and I sincerely apologize. In fact, the problem with me is that I am used to howling after eating anything. But please forget the past and let us make a new beginning. Come with me to enjoy the taste of tasty cucumbers. I promise that I shall not howl this time. Come with me and enjoy eating your fill. This time we are not going to that old farm. I have seen a farm across the river; we shall go there."

The poor camel was very simple and innocent. Once again the jackal managed to coax him and go across the river to eat cucumbers with him. And once again the jackal ate his fill quickly and returned to his old habit of howling. The guard of the farm heard him howling and came running with a big stick in his hand. The jackal took advantage of his small size and disappeared from the scene. But poor camel was trapped! He could not make his escape. And the result was that the camel was once again beaten thoroughly.

The camel was badly injured and he decided, much against his nature, that he would teach the wretched jackal a lesson. So, while on their return, the jackal was riding his back as usual and the camel was crossing the river and was in midstream, an idea suddenly flashed across his mind. He began weltering and rolling.

"Brother camel! What are you doing? I shall get drowned. Don't do this to me please," said the jackal nervously.

"Brother! Whether you drown or survive; I am not bothered about it. The problem with me is that when I see water after being beaten, I get an impulse to roll and toss about in the waves." Saying this the camel began rolling on his back in the river. And the wretched jackal was taken away by the restless waves of the river. Thus, the jackal got what he rightly deserved.

❏ ❏

19

SARCASTIC REMARK

There was a farmer. He was very hard working, and dashing by nature. In fact, it will not be wrong to say that it was his dashing nature and courage which carved his destiny and made him prosper. He had two sons who were very loyal to him and they took great care to see that their father did not suffer on any account. The elder son's wife was no less sincere to him.

One day he fell ill, and despite his son's and the daughter-in-law's best efforts, and despite the availability of best doctors of the town, the unfortunate day arrived and he breathed his last.

Now the entire responsibility of running the administration of the house fell on the shoulders of Vijai Singh—the elder son. Vijai Singh loved his younger brother—Jeet Singh—very much. Jeet Singh also had great respect for his elder brother. Both the brothers were proud of each other. But Vijai's wife did not like Jeet Singh so much. She was of the view that Jeet should also understand his responsibility and share the burden of her husband in farming and in other household matters. Though there was no feeling of jealousy between the brothers, Vijai's wife always looked at him with scorn.

One day Jeet singh returned home from somewhere and asked his sister-in-law for food. She hissed at him and said, "Go, and help yourself in the kitchen; I am not your servant."

Jeet Singh didn't say anything. He quietly went to the kitchen and began eating. That day his sister-in-law had not added salt to the preparation deliberately. The very first morsel spoiled the taste of his mouth. Jeet could not control himself. He came out of the kitchen. He was very angry, but he spoke in a guarded language, "What's wrong with you, sister-in-law? You did not add salt to your preparation; there is no taste in the food."

"I am not your cook. Why don't you marry the princess of Vijaygarh, if you are so fond of dainty dishes?" his sister-in-law made a sarcastic remark.

Jeet Singh said, "So, this is what you want. All right! I shall fulfil your wish. I take a vow that I shall return home only after I have married the princess of Vijaygarh."

The very moment Jeet Singh left the house and went to Sambhar—the capital of Vijaygarh estate. It didn't take him time to reach the palace. He addressed the king with due honour and said to the king with his suppliant arms upraised, "Maharaj! I wish to serve you."

The king looked at Jeet Singh; a handsome, shapely, and strong young boy he was. The king was very much impressed by his appearance and punctiliousness. He appointed him his bodyguard and gave him a house to live in near the palace. Jeet was only too happy to get this job.

One day the king went out with some dignitaries to the forest to hunt wild games. Chasing an antelope, the king went so far and at such a speed that none except Jeet Singh could manage to keep pace with him. The king and Jeet had come quite a distance in the dense area of the forest.

By now the king was completely exhausted. He took shelter in the shade of a tree to relax. Soon he fell asleep. There were many very dangerous wild animals in the forest. So, Jeet Singh unsheathed his sword and began guarding the king attentively.

Suddenly a tiger appeared from behind the bushes and roared loudly. The ear-splitting sound of the tiger's roar caused the king to wake up suddenly. But before the king could understand anything, the tiger leapt at him. Jeet Singh, who was already very alert and attentive, jumped in between the king and the tiger and engaged himself in a fierce fight with the tiger.

Both were fighting for life. After a brief fierce fight, Jeet Singh killed the tiger tearing its stomach with his sword. The tiger gave a ear-splitting roar and fell dead. But by this time Jeet Singh too had been injured so badly in the brief scuffle that he also dropped down unconscious.

Tears welled up in the eyes of the king to see the loyalty of his bodyguard. He somehow managed to bring him to the capital and ordered the royal doctor to administer medicines and cure him.

For many days there was no sign of improvement in the condition of Jeet Singh. People had begun thinking that he wouldn't survive; but everyone was praying wholeheartedly for him.

The king and the queen had developed a great liking and affection for him. They were extremely worried about Jeet Singh. Apart from the royal couple, the princess too was worried about him, because during all these days she had become a silent admirer of Jeet Singh and had put him on a high pedestal in her heart.

Anyway...ultimately God listened to the prayers of everyone and responded to the sincere efforts of the royal doctor, and Jeet Singh began showing signs of life. There was a wave of happiness all over. Gradual recovery and proper care filled him with vital energy in a short time. One day the king called him near and said, "Jeet! You did not even care for your life in trying to save me from the jaws of death. I wish I had appropriate words to thank you for your loyalty and sacrifice. I am filled with deep sense of gratitude for this act of yours. I wish to do something for you in return, but I am not able to decide. Could you yourself suggest to me something?"

Jeet Singh said, "Maharaj! I have only done my duty. It is the duty of a servant to sacrifice his life for his master, even hundreds of times, if required."

Hearing his brave bodyguard, the king became very happy.

The king thought for a while and said, "I think there is only one way I can compensate your sacrifice, and that is—give the hand of the princess to you in marriage. Is that acceptable to you?"

"It is my solemn duty to obey every order given by your Lordship. A king is considered the father of his subjects; and a father always thinks of the welfare of his children. What more can I say, Maharaj?"

The king became so happy with Jeet Singh that he immediately announced before his courtiers that he had selected Jeet Singh his son-in-law. The subjects also welcomed king's declaration open-heartedly. The courtiers also expressed their acceptance towards king's declaration.

One day Jeet Singh came to the king and made a strange request.

"Maharaj! I don't want gold, silver or other expensive ornaments in dowry. I want only one thing in the form of dowry."

"What is it?" the king was surprised.

Jeet Singh said, "Maharaj! I shall be extremely grateful to you, if you give me hundred camels laden with sacks of salt in the form of dowry.

The king and the queen, both, were greatly surprised at this strange demand. But when they realised that Jeet Singh was adamant to take only salt in dowry, they gave their acceptance. And then, on an aus-picious day, Jeet Singh and the princess were married to each other.

After that he sent a message to his brother that he would be returning home with his wife in a few days' time.

It had been many years since he had left his house. Vijai Singh's happiness knew no bounds when he learned that his brother was returning home after so many years. The day came when Jeet Singh came home. Both the brothers embraced each other with love and tears welled up in their eyes. Jeet Singh went to his sister-in-law's room with his wife and touched her feet with respect. He said, "This is my wife—the princess of Vijaygarh. She will help you in every household job. Apart from all this, I have been given so much salt in dowry that its stock won't exhaust throughtout our lives."

Hearing this Jeet Singh's sister-in-law began weeping. Now she was repenting for what she had said years ago. But Jeet Singh said, "Sister-in-law! Please don't feel sorry. I am indeed very grateful to you for that sarcastic remark. Had you not made that remark, the princess of Vijaygarh would not have become my wife. Someone has correctly said—whatever God does is always in favour of us."

❑ ❑

20

NATURAL BALANCE

ONCE a saint was touring different places with his disciples. One day, wandering with his disciples, he reached a village. Since the sun had set and it was getting dark, he went to the shop of a blacksmith and requested him to allow them some place where they could sleep in the night. The blacksmith extended wholehearted hospitality to the saint and his disciples. He offered them meals and gave them sufficient place to sleep in his house. He said to the saint, "Lord! I beg your forgiveness if there has been any inconvenience to any of you in my house."

The saint said, "My son! We are very happy with your hospitality, and I grant you three boons. You may ask for anything."

First the blacksmith hesitated and then he said, "Lord! If you do wish to give me something, kindly grant me a life of hundred years."

"So be it!" said the saint. "Now what's your second wish?"

The blacksmith was always worried about getting business orders. So, he wished that there should be no dearth of business orders.

The saint granted him the second boon also, and asked him to make his third wish.

The blacksmith could not immediately think of anything to make his third wish. So, he said, "Lord! Anyone who sits in this chair, in which you are sitting, should get stuck to it, and should not be able to leave it, unless desired by me."

The saint left the chair and said, "So be it!" and left with his disciples.

The boons of the saint came true one by one. The friends and relatives of the blacksmith died one after the other in due course of time, but the blacksmith remained as healthy as ever. He also had no scarcity of business orders. He used to sing all day and do his work happily. But no one on earth is immortal. Everyone has his final day one day. The blacksmith also completed his hundred years, and the final day arrived. The god of death came and stood at his gate, and asked him to go with him. First the blacksmith became very nervous, but then he said, "You are welcome, O Lord of Death! Please sit in this chair. Meanwhile, allow me to arrange my tools in proper order."

As soon as the god of death sat in the chair, the blacksmith roared into laughter and said, "Now you are stuck to the chair and cannot leave it without my permission."

The god of death began wriggling about in the chair, but could not free himself. The blacksmith left him there and went away giggling about his awkward situation.

Thinking that the god of death was in his captivity, the blacksmith became very happy. He thought of having a nice meal. He decided to cook chicken for himself. But as soon as he beheaded the chicken, the neck of the chicken automatically got fixed in its body; it returned to its original form and fluttered away.

The blacksmith ran after the chicken but could not catch it. Then he slaughtered a goat, but surprisingly the goat also returned to its original form and ran away. Now the blacksmith understood the mystery behind the sequence of happenings. He struck his forehead with his hand and said, "What a fool am I? When the god of death is in my captivity, how can anyone die? Well! Not bad! At least there won't be unpleasantness of death on the earth any more. I can manage with vegetarian meals, but at least my life will be secured." But by the end of the year the whole world began facing great difficulties. Because no human beings, no animals, no birds, and no insects died, and the number of creatures began increasing. Millions and millions of mosquitoes, flies, insects, rats, and frogs were born, but none died. These creatures began causing harm to farms also.

The birds ate all the fruits of the trees. The rivers and oceans became so full of fish, frogs, and other creatures that the water began stinking, and it was no more potable.

The sky looked black with locusts and mosquitoes flying all around. Dreadful snakes and wild beasts were loitering freely. Nature had lost its balance. Now everyone was in trouble. There was complete chaos all over.

Seeing such imbalance, the blacksmith realised his mistake. Now he realised that nature was incomplete without death; death was essential for keeping the nature in perfect balance.

The blacksmith came home in great speed and freed the god of death. The god of death fastened his noose around his neck and took him away with him.

After that everything became normal gradually. Creatures began dying and the nature began retrieving its balance.

❏ ❏

21

PRACTICAL EXPERIENCE

A very long time ago, there was a village which touched the borders of a desert. The lands of that village were very fertile. And since the lands yielded very good crops, the villagers enjoyed every happiness and prosperity. Once what happened that unfortunately it did not rain throughout the year; not a single drop of water. The village was severely hit by famine. All the wells and ponds went dry. The crops also died for want of water. Once very happy villagers, began dying of scarcity of water and food. The condition of the animals in the village was even worse.

One day the villagers decided to sit and discuss ways to counter the situation. They went to the chief of the village and requested him to hold a meeting in this regard.

The chief of the village was an elderly person. He was far-sighted and wise. It was for this reason that the villagers respected him a lot.

When the meeting started, a young boy stood and said to the chief, "Chief! You are already aware that the whole village has been undergoing very difficult problems. The situation is very typical. There is scarcity of food and water both, in the village. Already the animals were dying for want of fodder and water, and now the villagers have also started dying. Everyday you can see some bodies being cremated in the cremation ground. If it continues in this manner, a day will come when there will be none left in the village. There will be complete devastation."

The chief listened to him patiently and said, "Brothers! Situation is indeed very grim. But all of you, please have patience. Don't get disappointed. I am trying to find some way out. In fact, I had been thinking over this matter even before the meeting was called to combat the situation."

"Chief!" A young boy stood and spoke in a frisson of excitement, "I feel, by the time you reach a decision, half of the village would have been swallowed by the god of death. So, please stop thinking and do something."

"Listen, young boy!" said the chief calmly. "You are young and inexperienced, and so you are talking like this. Just imagine! I too am undergoing the same circumstances; I too have a family. I am also able to understand the grimness of situation; but I personally feel that one must consider all the aspects before finally coming to any decision. A hurried decision always leads to failures. So, no matter how big a problem is, one must not lose patience; one must not take steps that may leave him repenting throughout the life. Remember! there is always more than one solution to any problem. The biggest problems can be solved with understanding and wisdom."

The discourse of the chief had different effects on different people in the village. Most of the villagers agreed with the chief, but there were some who were so impatient that it seemed cowardly to them to talk of patience at that hour of crisis.

A very rash type of young boy whose blood was boiling with anger, suddenly spoke in a paroxysm of rage—"Chief! This is too much! You are teaching us to have patience at this hour of crisis? How to have patience? Do you mean to say that we should commit suicide? Now this is more than too much. We shall have to decide on our own."

Again the chief spoke very calmly, "Please be quiet, young boy. Getting angry and excited like this is not going to serve any purpose. I don't mean to say that you should continue to stay in this village under these circumstances. But think at least for once! Where shall we go? What shall we do? We have to contemplate this point also. God knows how far we may have to travel. We have to make at least some preparation for it."

"Excuse me, chief!" said the young boy, "I and my friends can wait no more. We are leaving this village today only. All who wish to accompany us, are welcome."

Seeing the young boy so impatient the chief became very sad. The chief once again tried to inculcate his opinion in the mind of the young boy and said, "My son! Please don't take a rash decision; don't act hurriedly. Those who lose their mental equilibrium; those who act in a sudden frisson of excitement, are always exposed to failures."

"Come on, chief! Don't talk nonsense!" said the young boy a little dejected. "Now we are not going to follow your advices. Our's is a firm decision."

"Son! Once again I advise you to maintain your mental equilibrium. I am your chief. I can never give you a wrong advice. I admit, you are full of energy, you have got enthusiasm, you are intelligent also; but what you lack in is experience—practical experience. My children! Practical experience in life is very important."

But the young boy refused to listen to his arguments, and giving absurd logics to his villagers, he misguided them. The result was that many villagers agreed to go with him.

Those who were willing to go with the young boy, began loading their necessary articles on bullock-carts, and after a brief preparation they left the village. The chief and the other villagers saw them off with heavy hearts.

A few days after the villagers had left the village with the young boy, the chief said to village people who had stayed back—"Brothers! Now I feel that we shall have to leave this village, as famine is in its full swing. Though I, and am sure all of you, will also be feeling extremely sorry while leaving the village of our ancestors, there is no alternative. If we survive, we can always come back and reestablish ourselves in this village."

Everyone agreed to this proposal of the chief.

The chief further said, "Brothers! Please start making preparations for the journey from right now; because at this hour it will not be possible for us to assess the time and number of days it may take to reach the right place. And all of you are well aware that before we reach

a desired place, we shall have to cross a big desert; and water is hardly available in any desert in the world. So, it is advisable that all of us carry as much water in our bullock-carts as possible."

"Would it not be possible to dig small wells and extract water from them, wherever we halt. Because it will be unnecessary trouble carrying so much water with us," one of the villagers submitted his proposal.

"No, this will not be correct. Being tired in our long journey, it will not be easy for us to dig wells; and even otherwise, digging well in a desert will be foolish. I once again insist that it will be better if we carry as much water as possible with us. One may compromise with hunger to quite an extent and survive, but surviving without water is impossible."

"It sounds logical," said one of the villagers. Then they went to fetch water from a nearby pond, which had gone almost dry. But the villagers took as much water as they could from the pond, and filled their pitchers. They loaded pitchers of water and eatables on their bullock-carts and on a definite day, set out to an unknown destiny. They adopted the same route that had been taken earlier by other villagers with the young boy.

Gradually their village was left behind and ultimately they entered the desert. They would halt at suitable places in the evening, cook their meals, eat, and sleep. Next morning they would start thier journey again.

After a few days when their caravan reached the middle of the desert, they were greatly surprised to see another caravan advancing towards them from the opposite side. They began thinking—'why this caravan is heading towards the destination, which we have left for want of food and water?' Then they thought—'perhaps they have got disorientated and coming to us, expecting us to help them.'

But when the caravan reached near, the villagers were startled to see their strange appearance. They had veiled their faces with black cloth. They had poleaxes, spears and sticks in their hands. They had covered their bodies with leathers.

The chief became doubtful about them to see them in such form. He thought these people must be desert robbers. The chief immediately alerted his carvan.

They stopped their bullock-carts as soon as they reached near. One of them, who looked frightening and who seemed to be their chief, jumped out of the bullock-cart and came near them. He said, "Brothers! Who are you all? Where are you coming from; and what is your destination?"

The village chief said, "Our village has been hit by famine, and so we are going to some unknown destination, where we can settle down and survive."

"Why have you kept so many pitchers in your bullock-carts?What is there in the pitchers?" the chief of robbers asked again.

"Brother! There is no water available in all the four directions in this desert. Having foreseen this problem we decided to carry water with us. These pitchers are filled with water."

"This is a desert; it is full of sand. I am sure you are aware that this sandy area is too difficult to be trodden by bullocks. How will they move with such heavy pitchers loaded on the carts?"

"That's our helplessness, brother. How shall we survive without water?"

"But there is no wisdom in what you are doing. If you keep moving thus it will take you years to cross this desert," said the chief of robbers showing his sympathy unnecessarily.

"Then what should we do?" said the village chief. "You yourself suggest to us some way."

"Personally I would suggest to you all to throw away the water and lessen the unnecessary burden," said the chief of robbers. "Once you have lessened your burden, the bullocks will start moving fast, and thus you will cross this desert early."

"Thanks for your advice, but I am sorry, we cannot follow it. In the absence of water we shall have lost our hopes of survival," said the village chief firmly.

"You people seem to be real fools! Brother! Don't you see it is raining havily on the other side of the desert? There is no dearth of water there. Look at us! Our clothes are still wet," the chief of robbers admonished the village chief.

"Rain in the desert? I am not able to believe your words," said the village chief.

"It's upto you. Believe it or not; but it is true that there is a dense forest on the other side of this desert. It's raining heavily there. So, this is for the last time I am telling you—Listen to my sincere advice; throw away the water from your pitchers; cross this desert as early as possible, and get rid of it. After all why carry unnecessary burden?"

Hearing him, the village chief became sure that that was a gang of cheats or of robbers, because no matter how wet one's clothes may be, it doesn't take time to dry in a desert. Then why are their clothes still so wet? What does that mean?

Seeing the village chief lost in thoughts, the chief of robbers said, "What happened, sir? What are you thinking? It's still not too late. Listen to my advice and throw away this unnecessary burden."

On this the village chief said, "Listen, brother! We have heard you. Now we shall decide our course of action among ourselves. I thank you for the kind sympathy shown by you."

Getting a straightforward reply from the village chief, the chief of robbers went away from there along with his band. Then the village chief said to his friends, "Brothers! I can see that some of my friends were very much impressed by the suggestion that we should throw away our stock of water and lessen our burden, so that we could cross this desert at the earliest. But I alert you—It will be self-defeating and ultimately suicidal to ignore my warnings. You perhaps don't know them. They are only trying to mislead us."

"How?"

"Brothers! They are desert robbers. When they get people in ones and twos, they rob them. But because we are more in number and we have got weapons also, they could not dare challenge us. They wanted to make us weak and kill our energy. Water is like nectar to us in this desert, and that's the reason why they were advising us to throw away our only hope of life, so that when we start dying of thirst, they could attack and plunder us."

The logical discourse of the village chief convinced the villagers of his caravan. Now they were proud of the wisdom of their chief. Those, who had become convinced of what the chief of robbers had said, had realised their mistake.

Then the village chief said, "Friends! We should not allow ourselves to be misguided by others. A stranger is always a stranger; we should not trust them blindly. There is great strength in unity; and we have to maintain it. We are going through a difficult situation, but this is only a temporary phase. Happy days will return to our lives once again. Getting nervous under difficult circumstances is cowardly. Bravery lies in facing problems courageously. Some of our friends had left our village in a hurry, and now I am worried about them. May God save them."

"Could something wrong happen to them?" One of the villagers said.

"In this frightening desert, where robbers are prowling throughout in search of their prey, anything could happen," replied the village chief.

The caravan began advancing again.

After going quite a distance, they saw a forest.

As if everyone was filled with new kind of life. They increased their speed moving in that direction. When they reached near they were surprised to see that there was no sign of rain. Now they realised how the stranger had lied to them. But they had at least this satisfaction that even if they didn't get rains, they would be able to relax in the shade of trees.

Suddenly one of them noticed a heap of something at a distance. He went near to check it, and what he saw was enough to fill anyone with horror. He screamed—"O my God! Friends! Please come and see."

Everyone ran in that direction. They were terribly frightened to see dead bodies strewn around. They began weeping bitterly. These were the dead bodies of those villagers who had refused to listen to the village chief and set out to find a suitable place for survival. Some of the dead ones were the relatives of those who had come with the village chief. Seeing their dead bodies, the village chief said, "It seems the whole caravan has been sacrificed on the altar of the goddess of the desert. Our poor brothers must have died of thirst."

The village chief consoled them and then they cremated the dead bodies in the desert itself. The village chief said in a sad tone, "Those who do not take advantage of the experiences of their elders, those who do not listen to good and sincere advices of their elders, always face such consequences,. Alas! They had listened to me. Just because they were less in number, they became an easy target of these robbers. I wish all of you take a lesson from this sad happening. Never let your unity be hampered. These robbers would have made us also their prey, had we not been united."

Everyone upheld the views of the village chief.

❏ ❏

22

THREE CUNNING BROTHERS

THERE lived three brothers in a village. They had remarkable deftness in fabricating stories. There stories used to be full of impossible events. Once these three brothers set out on a journey. When the sun set, and it started becoming dark and they were still half way to go, they decided to halt in an inn. A prince had also halted there. He was wearing expensive garments studded with gems and diamonds.

These brothers had never seen a prince; so seeing the prince they became very jealous of him. They thought why not make a fool of the prince also by fabricating some impossible stories.

They came to the prince and said, "Wouldn't it be nice for all of us to tell one story each and make the evening enjoyable?"

The prince liked this idea.

Immediately one of the brothers said, "Anyone of us who doesn't believe the story told by any of us, will become a slave of the one who was telling the story."

They selected and made an elderly person of the inn, a judge in order to announce his judgement in the event of disagreement on any point. They were confident that hearing their fabricated stories, full of impossible events, the prince will definitely express his disbelief, and either he will agree to become their slave or, in order to avoid becoming a slave, he will give some valuable things to them as penalty.

Some others, staying in the inn, also joined them, and sat around them to enjoy hearing stories. The eldest brother stood and began telling his story—

"When I was very young, I was very fond of playing the game of 'thief and police.' One day, while playing, I climbed a tall tree and hid myself in it. My brothers began searching for me. They kept looking around but couldn't find me. When it began getting dark, they gave up and returned disappointed. Now the problem before me was that I had to climb down, and by now it had become so dark that I could hardly see anything. So, I went to a nearby village and brought a rope from a hut. With the help of the rope I managed to come down without any problem and returned home safely."

The prince heard this baseless story but didn't say anything. He simply smiled and began waiting for the other one to start telling his story. The other two brothers were surprised that the prince had easily believed their eldest brother's story and didn't raise any question.

Anyway...the second brother began telling his story—

"That evening, when we were searching for our brother, who was hiding in a tree, I heard the rustle of something moving furtively in the bushes. I thought my brother was hiding there. I rushed in that direction, but surprisingly a dangerous and hungry lion appeared from behind the bushes. He had hardly opened his jaws when I dived into his mouth with lightning speed. I did all this at such a great speed that the lion could not get a chance to chew me. I had entered his stomach unscathed. Now I began jumping around, and I created so much problem for him that the lion began weeping with pain. Ultimately, in order to get rid of me, the lion regurgitated me, and that too with so much power that I was catapulted to my village, some two hundred miles away from there. I dusted myself and stood erect, as if nothing had happened to me. And thus I saved the villagers from the dangers of that lion. And the lion was so frightened that he never dared come to that village ever in his life."

Hearing this story also, the prince didn't say anything. He began looking at the third brother with a smile, waiting for him also to start telling his story.

The third brother was stunned to see how the prince had digested a story beyond logic. He began telling his story hesitatingly—

"One day I was taking a stroll along the bank of a river. I saw that all the fishermen were looking towards the river with disappointment. When I enquired about their plight, they said that they hadn't been able to catch a single fish during the entire week. Since they had not been able to earn a single penny, their family members were starving. I decided to help them and dived into the river. Apart from helping them I also wanted to know why these fishermen had not been able to catch a single fish in seven days. I had hardly gone a little distance towards the bed of the river when I saw a giant fish moving freely and looking for its prey. And the small fish were trying to hide themselves in different corners of the river. Now I understood why these poor fishermen had not been able to catch any fish during this period. This gaint fish had eaten away a majority of fish in the river. I immediately transformed myself into a fish and began advancing towards the giant fish. The giant fish began chasing me, and in this process she reached near the bank of the river. The fishermen were already waiting there for this fish with long spears in their hands. All of them attacked the fish and killed it. I was happy that I was able to help them and that their families won't starve any more. I transformed myself back into human form. All the fishermen and the villagers became very happy with me and they bid me farewell with lots of very costly gifts."

All the three brothers got very nonplussed to see that the prince had remained absolutely indifferent even after hearing the third story which was also full of impossible events. So, cunning as they were, these three brothers signalled to each other silently that they too would remain indifferent and won't make any queries no matter how unbelievable the story of the prince may be.

The prince started his story thus—

"I am a prince. There is no end to my property. I have come out in search of all the three slaves of mine who have suddenly absconded from my palace. I was also very fond of those three slaves, and that's the reason why I have been wandering in search of them. In a way I had lost all my hopes, but accidently I happened to meet them today. And now my search has come to an end, as fortunately I have been able to get my slaves back. And do you know who those slaves are? You three brothers!"

Hearing the story of the prince they were overcome by a kind of stupor. They were trapped in their own trickery. Now the situation was that if they refused to believe his story, they would lose, and even believing the story would make them his slaves. They became very nervous.

Then the judge announced his judgement in favour of the prince and declared that he had won the bet, and that it was incumbent on the three brothers to accept his slavery.

The prince had a hearty laugh to see them in this funny situation. He freed these cunning brothers on condition that in future they should not try to trap simple and innocent people in their fabricated and unbelievable stories.

The three brothers promised to restrain themselves from such activities, and thus saved their lives from slavery.

From that day onwards none heard these brothers telling false and baseless stories.

❏ ❏